"*Meade?*" Brooke asked in a stunned voice.

Meade's brows went up. "Was I *that* uncivilized last night?"

What she'd expected to find standing outside her apartment was a slightly tidied-up version of the academic adventurer she'd met in the wee hours of the morning. What she got was an impeccably elegant man in a Savile Row suit holding a lush bouquet of flowers. "No—no! Of course not. You just, ah, you . . . you look d-different."

Meade's teeth were a dazzling white against his sun-darkened skin. "You look different, too, Brooke," he said quietly, his brilliant, sky-colored gaze flowing over her.

Brooke shifted a little, one hand going up to finger the strand of pearls around her throat. Her brain and bloodstream seemed to be fizzing with the shock of his transformation. She felt as though she'd been transfused with champagne.

"Is—is there something I can do for you?" she asked after several moments of what struck her as very awkward silence.

The magnitude of Meade's smile suggested that this was a very loaded question . . .

Carole Buck

Born on the Fourth of July, Carole Buck was raised in Connecticut and now makes her home in Atlanta. Although she had ambitions to be a ballerina, a lawyer, an archaeologist, and a spy, she somehow ended up as a television news writer and entertainment reporter. She spends a lot of time in the dark, because she is also a movie reviewer. Her greatest fantasy is to travel back in time.

Carole is single. She says her men friends are always offering to help her do research for her romance novels. Her women friends want introductions to the heroes she writes about. Carole just wishes her characters would remember she's supposed to be in charge.

Life, says Carole, is a banquet, and she intends to fill her plate to the fullest as many times as she can.

Other Second Chance at Love books by
Carole Buck

ENCORE #219
INTRUDER'S KISS #246
AT LONG LAST LOVE #261
LOVE PLAY #269
FALLEN ANGEL #289
MR. OCTOBER #317
SWANN'S SONG #334
HAPPILY EVER AFTER #350
CODY'S HONOR #359
CHASING RAINBOWS #410
ALL THAT JAZZ #424
RAINBOW'S END #436
THE REAL THING #448

Dear Reader:

Along with warmer weather and lightening sky, March brings you *Window on Tomorrow* (#458), the third book in Joan Hohl's wonderful trilogy, and classic Second Chance at Love author Carole Buck's *Simply Magic* (#459).

You've met Andrea Trask as a witness to the loves of her roommates in *Window on Yesterday* (#450) and *Window on Today* (#454). Now Andrea faces a love that challenges the tests of time—and place! When Andrea sees her new earth-studies professor, she knows he's perfect, the man of her dreams—literally! But in fact, she's not dreaming. Her fantasy and gorgeous Paul Hellka are one and the same. After class discussions lead to soulful talks and long walks, Andrea finds herself still holding back. Although Paul is as ideal in reality as he was in her fantasies, something's not quite right. There's something mysterious about this dream-come-true that Andrea can't figure out. *Window on Tomorrow* (#458) is an ambitious adventure that will leave you full of wonder.

From the author of *The Real Thing* (#448), *Simply Magic* (#459) introduces a uniquely enticing hero, Dr. Archimedes Xavier "Meade" O'Malley. Awakened by strange music from the apartment below, Brooke Livingstone suddenly believes all the tall tales she's heard about her anthropologist neighbor, Dr. O'Malley. One strange meeting confirms those tales: he's intelligent, eccentric, charming, and handsome. And now he's interested in Brooke. Drawn to him as she is, it's still going to take a lot more than shared interests and spine-tingling passion to capture Brooke's disillusioned heart. Shattered dreams still fresh, Brooke harbors a painful secret. Have no fear—if anyone can show Brooke that time heals all wounds, that true love *is* simply magic, Meade O'Malley can...

Also from Berkley this month is *New York Times* bestselling author Cynthia Freeman's *The Last Princess*, an Alternate Selection of the Literary Guild and a Main Selection of the Doubleday Book Club. Lily had almost everything she desired, and yet, on the eve of her wedding, she threw it all away—for the love of another man. Harry Kohle was everything her parents despised, but Lily knew she couldn't resist Harry's love. From the high society of New York's Upper East Side, to the corrupting glamour of Hollywood, to the haunting beauty of Israel, their love faced the ultimate tests of hardship, struggle, and betrayal.

March also brings a spectacular novel by another *New York Times* bestselling author, LaVyrle Spencer. In the tradition of *Vows* and *The Gamble* is *The Hellion.* They were two loves, two worlds apart. Rachel is at the pinnacle of elegance, social standing, and beauty—when the wildest, most passionate flame of her youth steps into her life again. Tommy Lee's the all-time hell-raiser of Russellville, Alabama, with three marriages behind him and a string of fast cars and women. The townsfolk say he'll never change. But Rachel knows differently. Finally, don't miss *Silk and Satin* by author Marcia Wolfson. It's the story of a simple young woman seduced by the world of the wealthy, who must draw her strength from the one man most dangerous to her—the detective out to prove her guilt in the murder of her millionaire husband. From glass-walled boardrooms and Fire Island hideaways, to East Side watering holes and back room deal makers, *Silk and Satin* holds you in its glamorous grip until the shocking climax!

Don't miss these fabulous offerings—which are sure to chase any remnant chill from winter's weather—from some of the most accomplished writers on the romance scene today.

Until next month, enjoy and...

Happy reading!

Hillary Cige, Editor
SECOND CHANCE AT LOVE
The Berkley Publishing Group
200 Madison Avenue
New York, NY 10016

SECOND CHANCE AT LOVE™

CAROLE BUCK

SIMPLY MAGIC

BERKLEY BOOKS, NEW YORK

SIMPLY MAGIC

First edition published March 1989

ISBN: 0-425-11463-5

Second Chance at Love books are published by
The Berkley Publishing Group
200 Madison Avenue, New York, NY 10016

Printed in the United States of America

10 9 8 7 6 5 4 3 2 1

Chapter 1

THE NIGHT WAS HOT. AND so, in a hauntingly primitive way, was the music coming from the apartment beneath Brooke Livingstone's.

Drums . . . mimicking the rhythmic beat of the human heart.

Flutes . . . piping an oddly atonal yet insinuating melody that seemed designed to arouse the singing of the human bloodstream.

It wasn't being played all that loudly. But that, Brooke thought irritably, might be why it was having such an insidious effect on her. Plain old noise—the shriek of a fire siren, or the rock-and-roll blast from some kid's power radio—she could have blocked out by sheer force of will. But this—

Singing? Was someone singing now?

Brooke rolled over from her stomach onto her back and stuck her fingers in her ears. It didn't really do much good. Oh, true, she could barely hear the music, but she could still *feel* it. It was as though she was . . . was . . . It was as though she was *absorbing* the sound through her pores!

Brooke stared up at the ceiling, trying to ignore the unsettling sensations stirring within her. The music had started, without warning, about a half hour before, and the effects of it seemed to be intensifying with each passing minute.

She hadn't expected peaceful slumber to come easily tonight. To begin with, she was a bit overwrought after spending a rather tense Memorial Day weekend with her family in Connecticut. And, at the same time, Boston—like much of the rest of New England—was in the grip of an unseasonable heat wave, and the air-conditioning unit in her bedroom was on the fritz. This meant she had to contend with physical as well as emotional discomfort. Add those two factors to this all-too-disturbing music . . .

Brooke glanced at the clock-radio on the small, chintz-draped table next to her bed—it was past midnight. She had to be at work in the morning! If she didn't get some sleep soon, she was going to be exhausted. And, as understanding as her employer at the Wilding Institute for World Exploration—WIWE—was, she did *not* think he would appreciate her drowsing and drooping at her desk.

It had been her boss at the institute who had arranged for her to move into this gracious, high-ceilinged apartment in Cambridge when she'd arrived in Boston seven months before. The apartment occupied the spacious second floor of what had once been a two-story, single-family home. The present owner—presumably the source of the music—had had it converted, retaining the bottom floor for his own use while renting out the top.

Brooke had fallen in love with the elegantly old-fashioned house the moment she'd seen it and had been flabbergasted when she'd been told the monthly rent. The astonishing smallness of the quoted figure had been at least partially explained by the fact that whoever occupied the second floor was expected, in the owner's absence, to act as a sort of caretaker for the entire house and its handsomely landscaped yard.

Even with that proviso, Brooke had been more than willing to take the place. And, as it had turned out, her "caretaker" responsibilities had proven to be anything but onerous. Although she had to attend to her own housekeeping chores, there was a cleaning woman who dusted, polished, and vaccuumed the rest of the house once a week with awesome efficiency. There was also a pair of local teenage boys who had materialized to mow grass, rake leaves, or shovel snow as the need arose, for a small fee.

In truth, about the only thing Brooke was required to do was to collect her landlord's mail from the post office and lug it back to his residence. She'd been given a key to his front door, so she could deposit each day's load inside his apartment.

And "lug" and "load" were putting it mildly. Initially, Brooke had wondered why Dr. Archimedes Xavier "Meade" O'Malley didn't just have his mail delivered to his door. She'd stopped wondering after her first visit to the post office.

Brooke was fairly certain there were a lot of people who received less mail in their entire lifetimes than this one man received in a single week. Her landlord seemed to be in multilingual correspondence with several hundred people in several dozen different countries. He also appeared to subscribe to about a thousand publications and periodicals, ranging from the most obscure academic journals to several mass-circulation magazines that came in protective brown paper wrappers.

After sorting through O'Malley's mail for seven months—she couldn't just dump the stuff and run, after all!—Brooke thought she'd developed some insights into the kind of man he was. Of course, she'd also heard plenty about him from her colleagues at WIWE. Not that she believed more than a quarter of the stories she'd been told.

On the other hand, if just a fraction of the tales she'd heard of his swashbuckling scholarship were true . . .

She knew his area of expertise was ethnobotany, a field that combined anthropology and plant science. He'd spent years in the Amazon region studying Indian knowledge of medicinal plants and its applicability to the development of new drugs. When she'd rented the apartment, she'd been told he was in the South American rain forests and expected to remain there through August.

Brooke sat up, brushing impatiently at the fine cascade of fair hair that tumbled over her shoulders. Remain in the rain forests through August, hmm? Well, the last time she'd looked, August had been two full months away.

So much for what her landlord had been "expected" to do. Apparently, the man was back. Ahead of schedule. And he was downstairs playing music that seemed specifically aimed at driving her stark, raving crazy!

The rhythm of the drumming had changed . . . subtly, seductively. Brooke could feel her pulse dancing in response to it. The simple melody being played by the flutes had altered, too, becoming more and more inviting . . . more and more erotic—

That did it! Brooke kicked off the sheet, telling herself that the sudden hypersensitivity of her skin was due to the heat of the night and nothing else. *Nothing* else!

With a swing of her long, slim legs, she got off the bed. She was *not* going to spend the wee hours of the night being kept awake by the top ten musical hits from some academic adventurer's favorite primitive culture! She was going to march downstairs right this instant and tell her landlord what she thought of his inconsiderate behavior. Good Lord, the man hadn't even had the courtesy to come up, introduce himself, and tell her he'd returned home! And why he'd chosen to arrive by stealth in the middle of the night, she probably couldn't even imagine. Maybe he'd been hanging out with headhunters too long.

Brooke batted at her long hair once again. She found herself peculiarly—yet pleasurably—conscious of the caressing shift of it against her neck and shoulders. An odd feeling fluttered up and down her spine . . .

No! Brooke deliberately cut off this disturbing litany of physical awareness. She was hot and she was tired. Naturally, she felt a bit . . . a bit out of sorts. To read anything sexual into the sensations she was experiencing was absurd.

No, it was worse than absurd. It was pathetic. She, Brooke Livingstone, was a twenty-eight-year-old woman who hadn't been able to respond to her husband at all during the final six months of their marriage. She'd felt *nothing* but a deeper and deeper sense of physical estrangement. A deeper and deeper sense of personal failure. The notion that she was getting turned on by a piece of music was . . . was . . . unthinkable.

All she really needed was a good night's sleep. And it was obvious there was only one way she was going to get it.

Brooke reached for the celadon-green kimono lying on the foot of her bed. She knew precisely the tack she was going to take with Dr. A. X. O'Malley. She was going to be very polite, but very pointed. She was going to let him know exactly what she—

The music had changed again. Oh, no. The flutes had stopped, and someone—something?—was chanting. Brooke didn't have a clue about the language being used, but she had the distinct feeling that whatever entity or emotion was being invoked, it didn't involve rhyming words like "June," "moon," "croon," and "spoon." It was the most evocative melody she had ever heard.

She had to get that music shut off!

Archimedes Xavier "Meade" O'Malley was prowling around the book-crammed, artifact-cluttered living room of his apartment like a caged jungle cat. The primitive music throbbing from the cassette he had shoved into his state-of-the-art stereo system suited his restless, edgy mood very well.

Maybe too well. He probably should have gone with something soothing and civilized. Mozart, perhaps. The late Sebastian Browning, his longtime mentor and the man from whom he had inherited the house, as well as an extraordinary legacy of learning, had been of the opinion that listening to Mozart was the antidote for almost any emotional ailment.

Meade was acutely familiar with the restlessness he was feeling. He always went through this sense of dislocation when he got back from a stint in the field. It was part exhaustion, part culture shock, and part something else he'd never quite been able to put a name to. He knew that, after a day or two, he'd start feeling at home—or, at least, start feeling comfortable inside his own skin—again. But, until then . . .

Until then, he'd just have to accept the feeling that he was a stranger in a strange land.

Meade had arrived at Logan Airport, unheralded and unmet, about six hours before. His "welcome home" had been a sticky encounter with an extremely suspicious customs agent. Given the fact that either his looks or the contents of his luggage had conspired to get him hassled at nearly every major airport in the world at one time or another, the episode hadn't really been unexpected. But it had been a bit irritating.

Eventually, thanks to the intervention of a law-enforcement official who had recognized him from a previous trip, Meade had been spared the indignity of a strip-search, then sent on his way. After stuffing his belongings back into his bags and bidding an unfond farewell to the men of the U.S. Customs Service, he'd caught a cab into Boston.

After a brief internal debate, he'd decided against stopping by his parents' home to tell them he was back. There would be time enough to do that in the morning. It wasn't that he didn't care about his family or that they didn't care about him; quite the contrary. He just wasn't up to a full-scale reunion in his current mood.

And Meade knew, from repeated personal experiences, that a full-scale party was exactly what would have erupted if he'd turned up on his parents' doorstep. His mother, Eleni, would have wept, embraced him, then bustled off to telephone his twin sisters, Kathleen and Mary Margaret, plus every other person she could think of. His father, Francis, would have wept and embraced him, too, then offered him a bit of refreshment. Within a matter of minutes, the front doorbell would have been ringing and several dozen members of the Petrakis and O'Malley clans would have started pouring in. There would have been hugs and kisses, food and drink . . .

Drink. Oh, God. The prospect of the liquor alone explained why he felt the need to get himself reoriented before visiting his parents. During his time in the field, he'd drunk some of the most potent home-brewed booze in creation—purely out of scientific curiosity, of course. Okay, so, that wasn't entirely true. There had been two . . . mmm, maybe three . . . occasions when he'd held his nose and gulped down something because he'd sensed that to refuse would be to get himself killed by his insulted native host.

In any case, he'd imbibed alcoholic concoctions that had made moonshine seem like a soft drink. But *nothing* had ever gotten him more intoxicated—or left him with a worse hangover—than the alternate servings of whiskey and ouzo he inevitably was expected to swallow at family parties in order to acknowledge and honor his Irish and Greek heritages equally.

His mind darted briefly to the bottle of wine he'd picked up, along with two bags of basic foodstuffs and household necessities, when he'd gone out earlier. Maybe he should open it and have a glass or two. It might help relax him. Then again, it might not. In truth, he was no more in the mood to drink alone than he was to drink in the company of his kin.

Meade stopped pacing and stretched, trying to loosen the knots and kinks in the taut muscles of his back and shoulders. Raking his fingers through his thick, jet-black hair, he glanced around the room. His gaze settled on the orderly piles of mail sitting on the threadbare Persian rug in front of the fireplace, which dominated one wall of the living room. "B. Livingstone," according to the neatly lettered label on the mailbox at the front door, had done a fine job.

The upstairs apartment had been vacant when Meade had left for South America nearly eight months before on an expedition partially underwritten by the Wilding Institute for World Exploration. He'd asked the institute's executive director, Daniel Quincy, to find a suitable occupant. Meade trusted Quincy's judgment implicitly—despite the fact that the last tenant he'd recommended had come equipped with a pet boa constrictor named Ursula.

Not that Meade had had any objections to the snake. Ursula had been one of the most striking specimens of *Boidae* he'd ever run into, and he'd admired her as such. Unfortunately, she'd had a habit of sunning herself on the polished hardwood floor of the entrance hallway. Even more unfortunately, the woman he'd been involved with at the time had turned out to have an irrational, unshakable fear of snakes.

He'd felt some regret at the breakup, of course. But while he'd been fond of Jeanne, he hadn't loved her any more than she'd loved him. In fact, when all was said and done, he suspected that his matrimonially minded mother probably had been much more upset by the turn of events than he. More than that, she probably was *still* upset by it. As far as Meade knew, the major source of distress in his mother's life was that he was still unmarried at age thirty-five.

B. Livingstone. Barney? Benjamin? Bob?

The upstairs apartment had been dark when he'd arrived from the airport, but he'd gone up and knocked on the door anyway, just to be certain. There had been no response. He'd then gone downstairs, showered, shaved, and decided to go out to get something to eat. He'd returned about an hour and a half later, and checked the apartment once again. He'd thought, for a moment, that he'd heard something; but when no one had answered his knock, he'd shrugged and gone back down to his own place.

B. Livingstone. Bradley? Bernard?

Meade eyed the piles of mail thoughtfully, trying to decide what, if anything, he could determine from their orderly arrangement. That his new tenant was a man inclined toward—possibly obsessed with?—organization was obvious. And the fact that the mail had been sorted through so carefully suggested B. Livingstone might also be a rather inquisitive fellow. A . . . mmm . . . researcher. Yes. A researcher in one of the hard sciences. Probably brilliant in the lab but something of a disaster when it came to dealing with the real world. Physically—what? Short? Slight? Or, perhaps, tall and stoop-shouldered?

Glasses. He'd be willing to bet—

Meade's deductions were interrupted by the sound of someone knocking on his apartment door. He tensed at the sudden noise, his jungle-honed instincts taking over. A jolt of adrenaline poured into his system.

There was another knock, this one a bit more imperative than the first.

"Coming," Meade said sharply, and crossed the living room in long, lithe strides. He released the dead-bolt on the door and pulled it open.

The last thing he expected to see standing in front of him was a beautiful woman.

She was slender and wrapped in something made of silk. The garment—which was the color of spring leaves—embraced the graceful curves of her body like a lover. Her hair flowed, long and loose, over her shoulders. It was as pale as spun sunlight.

The features of her fair-skinned, oval face had the purity of a Madonna. Except for her mouth. The ripe shape of her lips spoke of very earthly passions.

Her wide-set, long-lashed eyes were green and guarded. They reminded him of a rain forest. A man could take every precaution in the world and still become utterly lost in them.

Meade stared. It was about the only thing he was capable of doing at the moment that didn't involve making a fool of himself.

Because institute gossip rated Meade O'Malley something of a lady-killer, Brooke had expected him to be attractive. She had not, however, expected him to look like a cross between a walk-the-plank pirate and a Greek god!

The man standing in the doorway was tall. Brooke stood five feet seven in her bare feet, and he topped her by at least six inches. His lean, powerful-looking body had an almost sculpted symmetry. He was clad only in a pair of low-riding khaki shorts. While the garment was badly frayed and a bit baggy, it could not disguise the virility of the man wearing it.

He had curly dark hair that looked as though it hadn't been properly cut—hacked at with a knife, maybe—in months. His sun-darkened skin had a warm, olive cast to it and sat taut over the strong bones of his face. She'd seen strongly compelling features like his carved on the statues of ancient Athenians.

But none of those potently perfect statues had had eyes the color of a sunlit sea. A woman, even with a Red Cross certificate in life-saving, could drown in Meade O'Malley's brilliant blue eyes . . . and probably enjoy the experience.

Brooke stared. It was either that or melt into a puddle on the floor.

Meade wasn't certain how long they stood there, studying each other. He had the feeling that the air around them was quivering, as though it had been charged by a lightning strike.

The music he had been playing ended in an urgent rush of drumbeats. The stereo system shut off with a barely audible click as the tape ran out. After a few seconds—minutes? hours?—of stunned silence, Meade spoke.

"Ah . . . B. Livingstone, I presume?" he inquired. As he heard the words coming out of his mouth, he was reminded of the old adage that if one kept quiet, one could only be *suspected* of being an idiot; whereas, if one spoke . . .

B. Livingstone, I presume? God! He hadn't used an opening line that lame since . . . since . . .

In all honesty, Meade didn't think he'd *ever* used an opening line that lame before. Never. Ever.

Brooke blinked. "I . . . ex-excuse me?" she replied, her words soft and uncertain. She felt as though her brain cells had been scrambled. Heaven only knew what had been done to the rest of her!

"Nothing," he said ruefully. "It was a very old joke. It doesn't bear repeating."

"An old joke—?" Brooke blinked again, trying to force whatever was left of her mind to start functioning in something approaching a coherent fashion. "Oh. You mean . . . what you said about presuming I'm Livingstone?"

"Exactly." He nodded, one corner of his mouth twisting into a smile. "I apologize. You've probably been hearing variations on that all your life."

Brooke shook her head. "Actually . . . no," she said slowly. "Livingstone is—was—my husband's name. That is, it's *still* his name. And mine, too. I mean, I kept it after he—we—you see, we—I'm not—" She could feel her cheeks flooding with hot, embarrassed color as she became more and more entangled. "We—we're divorced," she concluded baldly.

There was a short silence during which Brooke mentally berated herself. She believed in keeping her private life private. Her six-year marriage—a marriage that had begun so wonderfully and ended so woefully—was no one's business but her own. Yet, here she was, blurting out personal facts to a half-naked man she'd just met—

Spine stiffening, Brooke drew herself up. She crossed her silk-sleeved arms in front of her. She wasn't sure whether she was shutting herself in or shutting Meade O'Malley out. She simply felt an intense, instinctive need to erect some kind of barrier around herself.

"I'm . . . sorry," Meade said finally.

He didn't pursue the subject. It wasn't that he didn't want to learn more about this woman. He did. But he knew enough about body language to read the nonverbal NO TRESPASSING sign she'd just posted. This was not the time to ask questions.

He met her wary green gaze steadily, wordlessly trying to assure her that he was worthy of her trust. There were troubling shadows in the vibrant depths of her eyes.

Again, Meade thought of the rain forests he'd so recently left.

Although she couldn't rationally explain why she felt it was safe to do so, Brooke started to relax a bit. Some of the tension eased out of her posture and, after several seconds, she unfolded her arms and brought them slowly back down to her sides.

"I—ah—I'm Brooke Livingstone," she said at last. Her voice, she was relieved to hear, sounded fairly close to normal. "From . . . upstairs."

Brooke. The elegant simplicity of it suited her, Meade decided.

"Brooke Livingstone," he repeated, extending his hand. "I'm Archimedes Xavier O'Malley."

Brooke put out her own hand automatically. An instant later, his strong, callused fingers clasped her much more delicate ones.

The press of palm against palm was as intimate as a kiss.

"How . . . how do you do, Dr. O'Malley," Brooke said, trying to ignore the toe-curling thrill of physical response she was experiencing.

A simple touch wasn't enough to start the earth quaking for Meade, but he was damned sure he felt a tremor of reaction during the heady instant when he took Brooke's hand in his. Her skin was smooth and he was willing to wager it carried the scent of some sweetly perfumed lotion.

"Meade, please," he corrected. His voice was warm. His vivid blue eyes were more than that. "I usually go by Meade. Unless you prefer—" He said something in an exotic-sounding dialect.

Brooke took a deep breath, struggling to retain some semblance of control over herself—if not the situation. What was happening to her? And *why* was it happening to her?

"Ex-excuse me?" she inquired warily, withdrawing her hand from his with a curious combination of reluctance and relief.

He grinned, and for an instant, Brooke saw a disarming glimpse of the boy this formidable, emphatically adult man must once have been. "That's what the tribe I've been living with calls me," he explained. He was more than a little tempted to reclaim her hand, but decided not to press his luck. At least, not right yet.

"I see," Brooke returned, not completely sure that she did.

"It means 'very large outsider with skin like ugly frog underbelly.'"

Brooke was startled into laughter. "Oh . . . of course. That was going to be my first guess," she said lightly.

Somewhere in the back of her mind, a small voice advised that this was turning into a very peculiar conversation. Here she was, dressed for bed, standing in the doorway of the apartment of a semiclad man she barely knew, chatting away as though . . . as though . . . well, she didn't quite know *what*.

While Meade was accustomed to handling himself in strange situations, he was finding this encounter more and more disconcerting as it unfolded. Brooke Livingstone's gut-level effect on him was more powerful than anything he'd ever experienced. And it wasn't just his gut that was affected. Yet there was more to his response to her than just the sensual . . .

"Well, actually, that's the polite translation of it," he said, running a hand through his hair. "Look, uh, why don't you come in? It's really ridiculous for us to stand here talking like this—don't you think?"

"Ah—" Her hesitation involved more than her awareness of the hour and of the way they were both dressed—or undressed!

"Please . . . Brooke?" He watched her intently, trying to divine what she was thinking.

She glanced down at the floor for a moment, then back up at him again. "All right," she capitulated. "But I really can't stay very long."

"Fine," he agreed easily, stepping aside so she could enter. The fragrance of her skin teased him as she moved by. That delicately provocative scent plus the discreet sway of her hips beneath the silk of her robe made him recall his earlier, off-by-a-mile speculations. "B. Livingstone, indeed," he murmured under his breath.

Brooke turned to look at him, her fair hair swinging against her back. "Yes?" she questioned.

"Wha—? Oh." He realized she must have heard him

say her name. "I was just thinking about—you're not what I expected, you know." He closed the door.

Brooke wasn't certain how to react to this rather open-ended observation. He wasn't what she'd expected, either! "Really?" she responded after a moment. "What . . . what did you expect?"

Meade's mouth twisted wryly. "To tell you the truth—a nerd named Barney or Benjamin," he confessed.

"Excuse me?" Brooke said after a fractional pause.

"I saw the initial on the mailbox by the front door and I just assumed—" He stopped, remembering something. "Mail! God. I apologize. I should have thanked you for taking care of my mail all these months. I appreciate what you did very much. I hope it wasn't too much trouble."

"Oh, no," Brooke assured him. "Not at all." She hesitated for a moment, then picked up the thread of his initial comment. "So, you . . . assumed B. Livingstone was a man?"

"Among other things," he said with a self-deprecating shrug. "Let's just say I was guilty of forming a hypothesis using very inadequate data."

Brooke's brows came together. "Is it a problem for you?"

"What? Coming up with half-baked theories based on half-ass—excuse me—incomplete information?"

"No." She shook her head. "My . . . not being a man." Of course, she wasn't exactly the typical woman, either. But Archimedes Xavier O'Malley didn't know that. That was her secret. Hers and Peter's. She had no intention of sharing it with anyone else.

No intention. Ever.

For a second, Meade wondered if Brooke was being flirtatious. Her soft inquiry certainly sounded like a come-on. He was on the verge of replying in kind when he glimpsed something in the depths of her eyes that made him stop.

She wasn't being flirtatious. She was genuinely concerned. But why in heaven's name—?

"No," he answered. "It's not a problem."

There was a moment of silence then, part awkward, part assessing. Brooke was aware of him studying her, and it made her feel both uneasy and oddly excited.

She flushed a little and glanced away, brushing at her cornsilk-pale hair.

Meade realized he'd been staring. His brain felt hazy—as though he'd been drugged. He shook his dark head in an effort to clear it.

"Sorry," he apologized. What was it about this woman that was affecting him so strongly? "I don't know why—it must be jet lag. Flying from Brasilia to Boston is—ah—" He gestured.

Brooke looked at him, her earlier reservations reasserting themselves. "Maybe I should go," she said. "You must be tired after your trip. I didn't realize—" She made a small movement toward the door.

"No!" Meade objected sharply, reaching forward to catch and stop her. The tips of his fingers grazed her upper arm and he felt an electric shock at the contact.

He saw Brooke's green eyes—green eyes that seemed to hint at so many contradictions—widen, and knew she'd experienced the same physical jolt he had. She'd experienced it . . . yet she seemed almost afraid of it. Why?

"No," he repeated, moderating his tone. "Please, don't leave. Not yet. I—" Something suddenly occurred to him. Something which, he told himself, he really should have had the sense to ask about as soon as he'd opened the door and seen her.

"Look," he said firmly. "You can't go until you tell me why you came down here in the first place."

Brooke gazed at him blankly. "Why I— Oh! Yes. Why I came down here." It was more than a little disturbing to realize that, until he'd raised the subject, she'd completely forgotten her reason for pounding on his door. So much for her earlier plans about being polite, pointed, and perfectly clear! "I—it was the music you were playing," she explained awkwardly. "I wanted to . . . talk . . . to you about it."

It took Meade a second to figure out what she meant. Once he did, he felt like an idiot. An inconsiderate idiot.

"You mean you wanted to *complain* about it," he amended with a grimace. "Damn. I'm sorry, Brooke. I never would have—I didn't know you were upstairs. I checked twice—"

"You did?" Brooke interrupted. "When?"

He told her.

"Oh . . ."

"I knocked pretty loudly—"

"I'm sure you did," she assured him. "But I was away for the weekend—"

"Away?" he queried, not quite as casually as he'd intended.

"I was visiting my family in Connecticut," Brooke explained. She suppressed a small grimace. Why, oh why, she asked herself, had her mother and older sister insisted on performing yet another postmortem on her failed marriage? And why had they been so eager to tell her all about her ex-husband and his new wife? "I must have gotten back after the first time you came up. As for the second time you checked—" She calculated. "That had to have been while I was in the shower. I can't hear anything when the water's running." She paused, frowning slightly. "And I guess you didn't hear me when I knocked on your door—"

"I probably wasn't in. I went out for a while to get some supplies," he told her, wondering about the unhappy emotion he'd seen flicker across her face when she'd mentioned her family.

"Ah." Brooke's expression cleared as the final piece fell

into place. "In other words: Good intentions . . . bad timing."

"Exactly. Still, I apologize. I don't normally play my stereo full-blast at nearly one in the morning. But I was feeling a little wound up after my trip and I thought some music might—" He gestured, his blue eyes moving over her, traveling from her loose hair to her bare feet. "I obviously woke you up. I'm sorry."

"Actually—you didn't," Brooke said, fingering the sash of her robe. "I wasn't asleep. I was . . . my trip left me feeling a little wound up, too. Plus, the air conditioner in my bedroom isn't working. And then, well, when the music started . . ." She slanted him a glance. "You were listening to it to . . . relax?" she questioned dubiously, vividly recalling the unsettling sensations the music had evoked in her.

"Not exactly," Meade conceded. He decided this was not the time to tell her about the exact nature of the music he'd been playing. "It's hard to—I'm not even sure at this point why I put that particular tape on. But, again, I do apologize." He waited a beat. "Ah—going back to the supplies I mentioned before. I've got a bottle of wine in the refrigerator I was thinking about opening. Could I talk you into sharing it with me?"

Brooke had the distinct feeling that he could talk her into sharing a lot of things.

"I don't . . . it's late," she temporized, lifting one hand and using it to hook her hair back behind her ears. "I've got work in the morning—"

"Just one glass." There was a fine line between pushiness and persuasiveness, and Meade knew how to walk it like a tightrope artist. "It might help you fall asleep."

Brooke hesitated for a few more seconds, then indicated her acceptance with a dip of her head. She had a sense of surrendering to the inevitable. "Just *one* glass," she emphasized.

"Deal." His smile was warmly pleased and made the network of fine lines at the outer corners of his eyes crinkle. "Make yourself at home. I'll be right back." Pivoting on his heel, he headed off toward the kitchen with a supple, silent stride. As he turned away from her, Brooke caught a glimpse of what appeared to be an intricate red-and-black tattoo on his left shoulder blade.

And just how had he acquired that? she wondered, her imagination conjuring up all sorts of exotic possibilities. Now that she'd actually met Meade O'Malley, Brooke was convinced she'd been wrong to doubt so many of the stories she'd heard about him. At this moment, she was willing to believe every one of those tales was true—and then some!

Brooke glanced around. She'd been stunned by this room and its contents when she'd entered for the first time. Everywhere she looked, there were artifacts from cultures completely alien to her modern, twentieth-century mind. There were bizarrely beautiful masks and pieces of sculpture. Spears and shields. Blow guns and beadwork. And dozens and dozens of items she couldn't begin to identify. There were endless shelves of books as well, plus scores of silver-framed photographs scattered about.

That the room was compelling was not at all surprising. That it should strike Brooke as comfortable, too, bordered on the astonishing. Yet, inexplicably, it did.

"Here we go," Meade announced genially, advancing toward her with one of the two glasses of white wine he was carrying extended. His return to the room had been as noiseless as his exit.

Starting slightly at the sound of his quiet yet resonant voice, Brooke turned back to face him. Once again, she felt herself almost overwhelmed by the force of his masculine presence.

"Thank you," she said, accepting the proffered glass and taking a hasty sip of wine. "Ah—I hope you don't mind that I was looking around," she continued after a second or two.

"Not at all," Meade replied honestly. He took a much slower drink than Brooke had, studying her over the rim of his glass as he did so. The delicate complexity of the chilled Chardonnay seemed to complement and underscore the impressions he was forming of her.

That his new tenant was very, very appealing to look at was beyond dispute. Yet, as attractive as he found her physically, it was the qualities he sensed stirring beneath her lovely exterior that caught and held his interest.

Brooke veiled her eyes with her lashes for a few moments. She was, once again, very much conscious of Meade's assessment. Her ex-husband, Peter, had watched her without speaking, too. He'd been searching for flaws and, heaven knew, he'd found enough of them.

She could understand—all too well—why he'd done it. Peter had felt she'd failed him in almost every way a wife could fail a husband . . . almost every way a woman could fail a man. And, in the end, she'd felt the same way.

Because she *had* failed him . . .

Brooke took another swallow of wine, licking a stray drop of it from her lower lip with a quick dart of her tongue.

"This—this really is an extraordinary room," she commented, glancing around once again. "The first time I let myself in to drop off your mail, I thought I'd walked into a museum."

"You should have seen what it was like when Professor Browning was alive," Meade told her. "He willed the major part of his artifact collection to the university. Most of these things are . . . well, his personal souvenirs."

"Some of them must be yours, too." Brooke pursued the topic eagerly, partly because she was genuinely interested, partly because it seemed like a relatively safe subject. "I know you inherited the house from him. But, still—"

"The dance masks are mine," he acknowledged. "And the fetishes over there. I've got a special interest in tribal magic."

"Magic?" Brooke repeated. The word teased for a moment, then triggered an association. "I think I've heard—" She chased the connection and pinned it down. "Someone at the institute once mentioned something about your doing—ah—card tricks for cannibals?"

Meade chuckled, then shook his head. "I know some sleight-of-hand," he told her. "And, I've occasionally used it in the field. Frankly, it makes a better impression than flashing my doctoral dissertation. As for entertaining alleged cannibals—" He shook his head again. "Well, one of the tribes I've had contact with probably *did* roast up a couple of Spanish friars—pardon the pun—a few centuries ago, but I wouldn't hold it against them. After all, if you trace just about *anybody's* ancestors back far enough you'll find . . . ah . . ."

"Skeletons in the family pantry?" Brooke suggested delicately.

"Precisely," Meade concurred, his eyes glinting with appreciative amusement. "'Skeletons in the family pantry. . .' Nice turn of phrase. Would you mind if I quoted it?"

"Not if you put the proper citation in your footnotes," Brooke responded lightly. She was feeling increasingly at ease with Meade. She wasn't certain whether she should welcome her growing sense of relaxation or be wary of it.

"The proper—" His dark brows came together. "Hold on. You said something about 'the institute.' Do you work for WIWE?" He pronounced the acronym "whywee."

Brooke nodded. "Technically, I'm Daniel Quincy's executive assistant. But my job involves doing a lot of different things. Because I've got an undergrad degree in English and some university press experience, I've ended up red-penciling a few of the institute's recent monographs."

"Hmmm." His dark brows lifted. "In other words, I've got my own in-house editor?"

The question was half quip, half caress. Brooke decided she was better off not replying.

"You . . . mentioned Professor Browning a minute ago," she commented after a fractional pause. "I've heard so much about him. He must have been an amazing man."

It wasn't the smoothest change of subject Meade had ever heard; still, he accepted it for the same reason he'd resisted his earlier impulse to reclaim her hand after she'd withdrawn it from his.

"I think 'amazing' is a pretty fair assessment," he concurred.

"You were one of his students?"

"From the age of twelve."

"What?" Brooke was startled. While Archimedes O'Malley was routinely described as brilliant, she'd never heard any mention of his attending college at age twelve!

"That's how old I was when I met him," Meade explained. "My dad is—was, actually, he's retired—an electrical contractor. One afternoon, he brought me along on a job he was doing on the fourth floor of the Botanical Museum. I decided to explore and ended up in Professor Browning's lab. With things like blow pipes and spears lying around, I couldn't resist touching. I'd just picked up a stone arrowhead when this very British voice suddenly said: 'The poison on that can kill a jaguar in seconds, young man. Do try to be careful, won't you?'" Meade spoke the last two sentences in a *Masterpiece Theatre* accent.

"What—what did you do?"

"Oh, I was very, *very* careful!" Meade assured her with a grin. "I tried to play it cool, but I was scared out of my skin."

"I should think you would have been!" Brooke said, visualizing the scene. "Was there *really* poison—?"

"Oh, sure," he confirmed casually. "Curare. Professor Browning gave me a lecture on it. Once I recovered from my state of shock, I started asking questions. One thing led to another, and he wound up inviting me to visit him again." Meade paused, savoring some fond memories. "I don't think he expected I'd skip school and show up the next day, but I that's what I did. I was hooked. He was . . . one of a kind."

"These pictures—they're all of him?" Brooke walked over to a table near the fireplace that was cluttered with black-and-white photographs plus a collection of small stone and wood figurines. "I have to admit I've been curious about them."

As she leaned forward to take a better look at one particular photo, the wrapped front of her pale green robe gapped open slightly, revealing the soft upper swell of her breasts. Meade took a quick gulp of wine and shifted his glance.

"The woman is Gabrielle Browning, the professor's wife," he said, uncomfortably conscious of the effect she was having on him. "She was a lot younger than he was. She was killed in a car accident while he was out in the field doing research. Professor Browning . . . took it very hard."

Brooke brushed her fingertips gently against the frame of what obviously was a wedding portrait. The picture radiated life and love.

She could not help but envy the two people in the photograph the emotions they so plainly had shared in their time together. Had she and Peter ever looked—? Had they ever felt—?

After a moment, without really thinking about what she was doing, Brooke set down her wineglass and picked up one of the stone figurines from the table. It seemed surprisingly heavy for its size.

Surprisingly heavy . . . and oddly warm to the touch.

"What—?" she wondered aloud.

"It's pre-Columbian," he told her offhandedly. "It's supposed to ensure fertility."

Fertility.

Brooke went cold . . . inside and out.

"Oh," she said, staring at the small statuette, suddenly seeing the hopes embodied in its burgeoning curves.

To ensure fertility.

"Brooke?" Meade asked.

Slowly, carefully, she put the figurine back where she'd found it. A part of her wanted to throw it to the floor and see it shatter. But she knew that wouldn't help.

Nothing would help.

"Brooke? Are you all right?"

"I'm fine," she lied.

Chapter 2

BROOKE DIDN'T WANT TO THINK about it, but she couldn't seem to stop.

A fertility statue.

She grimaced at her reflection and jabbed another bobby pin in her upswept hair.

A fertility statue! Of all the artifacts in Meade O'Malley's apartment, *why* had she picked up that one? she asked herself for what was probably the thousandth time. What perverse instinct had drawn her to it?

To be a wife and mother was all she'd ever really wanted. Once upon a time, she'd believed both things were possible. No more.

She had met Peter Livingstone in her junior year of college and married him a month after her graduation. Hers had been a white-lace-and-orange-blossoms wedding—so traditional that several of her bridesmaids had teased her about it. But she hadn't minded. She believed in tradition . . . in old-fashioned values. Marrying the man she loved—building a life with him—had meant everything to her.

Peter had been eager to start a family. So had she. She

could remember them laughing about the possibility of her becoming pregnant on their honeymoon. Underneath the laughter had been a fondly held hope.

But she had not become pregnant on their honeymoon. Nor had she become pregnant during the first two years of their marriage.

Subtle pressure from her parents—and his—had started shortly after their second anniversary. There had been casual comments about other people's grandchildren and not-so-casual questions about when they might expect to have some of their own.

Brooke had been the one to propose consulting a fertility specialist. Peter had been angered by the idea at first, angered by what he saw as her suggestion that there might be something "wrong" with him as a man. It had been their first serious quarrel, and it had shown her a side of Peter that had made her uneasy. Eventually, however, he'd agreed to her request.

The doctor had been very kind, very compassionate, when he'd given them his diagnosis. He hadn't said "It's your fault" to Brooke, but that was what she'd heard. And that was what she'd seen when she'd looked into her husband's eyes.

She had been willing to try anything. Examinations by other specialists. Tests. Fertility drugs. Even an operation. There had been hurt. There had been humiliation. But there had been no help.

The physical side of her marriage had deteriorated. Suddenly the calendar dictated when she and Peter made love; instructions from medical experts governed the way in which they did so. Spontaneity died. The gentle preliminaries Brooke had treasured were discarded. Sex became a cold, joyless duty to be performed.

Then Peter had begun belittling her. At first, he'd only done it humorously and in private; but, after a time, he had done it in front of other people, too. He'd taken to saying that *he* was not the one to "blame" for their failure to have a family.

Brooke didn't know exactly when he'd stopped being faithful to her. She only knew that he had.

The end had come the evening of their sixth anniversary. Peter had come home late and a little drunk. She'd asked him where he'd been and he'd told her in graphically descriptive terms.

Why? he'd said. *You want to know why, Brooke? Because I'm a man and I can't get what I want—what I need—from you! You can't give me a son and you can't give me much satisfacton, either! You're not just infertile —you're frigid, too!*

That night—and the divorce that had followed—had left Brooke shattered. But, during the past year, she'd done her best to put herself back together. Coming to Boston had been a big and somewhat scary step. Still, it had been a step in the right direction . . . or so she'd thought until a little more than sixteen hours before.

And then she'd heard that insidious music.

And met the devastatingly attractive man who'd been playing it.

And picked up his damned—

The buzz of her apartment doorbell yanked Brooke out of the past and back into the present.

"Brooke?" an unmistakable male voice called.

Her pulse accelerated from a fast trot to a full gallop in the space of a second.

Another buzz.

"Brooke?"

"Just—just a minute!" she called.

Brooke gave her mirrored image a final once-over, then exited the bathroom. The heels of her strappy evening sandals clicked against the floor as she crossed to the front door. After taking a deep, steadying breath, she undid the locks and turned the knob.

What she expected to find standing outside her apartment was a slightly tidied-up version of the academic adventurer she'd met in the wee hours of the morning. What she got was an impeccably elegant man in a Savile Row suit holding a lush bouquet of flowers.

"Meade?" she asked in a stunned voice.

Meade's brows went up. "Was I *that* uncivilized last night?"

"Uncivil—?" Brooke echoed, scrabbling to regain some kind of equilibrium. It wasn't easy. "No—no! Of course not. You just, ah, you . . . you look d-different."

Different, indeed. The over-long dark hair had been expertly cut and faultlessly brushed and the baggy shorts had been replaced by a beautifully tailored navy suit. He looked like a candidate for the cover of *GQ* magazine, not a man who'd spent the better part of the past year in a jungle!

Meade's teeth were a dazzling white against his sun-darkened skin. "You look different, too, Brooke," he said quietly, his brilliant, sky-colored gaze flowing over her.

She was wearing a simple slip of a cocktail dress made out of a floaty, pale yellow fabric. Her blond hair was swept up in a modified Gibson Girl knot, and there were pearls at her throat and ears. The overall effect was ladylike—almost demurely proper. Yet Meade found it as provocative as the just-tumbled-out-of-bed impression she'd created at their first meeting.

Brooke shifted a little, one hand going up to finger the strand of pearls around her throat. Her brain and bloodstream seemed to be fizzing with the shock of his transformation. She felt as though she'd been transfused with champagne.

"Is—is there something I can do for you?" she asked after several moments of what struck her as very awkward silence.

His smile suggested that this was a loaded question.

"Well, first of all, you can accept these," he replied.

"These" were the flowers he was holding. He extended them to Brooke with a small flourish.

"But—but, why—?" she questioned, even as she was reaching out to take the proffered bunch of white and yellow blossoms. "I don't—"

"In appreciation for the mail and an apology for the music."

"Oh, no—" she started to protest.

"Please," he interrupted, raising one hand. "Don't tell me I didn't have to."

"Well, you didn't!" she returned immediately. The gesture was completely unnecessary. Unnecessary . . . yet very, very nice. "You didn't have to," she repeated firmly, then let her lips soften into a smile of genuine pleasure as she gazed down at the exquisite bouquet she'd been given. She looked up at him. "But . . . I'm glad you did," she admitted. "Thank you, Meade."

"You're welcome."

There was another brief pause.

"I should put these in water," Brooke said finally, wondering if she'd been staring at Meade as obviously as she felt she'd been. The lure of his blue eyes was as compelling as she remembered it. "Would you—would you like to come in for a few minutes?"

"Thanks."

"It can't be—actually, I'm, ah, leaving in a little while—"

"No problem. I'm going out soon, too."

"Oh." Brooke turned away, experiencing an unpleasant pang of emotion. So that was the reason for his extraordinary transformation. He was "going out."

"Brooke—" Meade started, then stopped as he got a look at the back of her dress. The neckline veed to a point between her shoulder blades, revealing a triangle of creamy-fair skin. The sight of this, plus the vulnerability of her bared nape, sent a sudden wave of heat through him.

"Yes?" Brooke asked, pivoting back to look at him.

In the hours following their first encounter, Meade had tried to tell himself that the potent response he'd had to Brooke essentially had been the product of nearly a year of sexual abstinence. He hadn't been with a woman—a matter of choice, not an absence of opportunity—since before he'd left Boston. So, it was perfectly understandable that, when confronted with a desirable female—*any desirable female*—he'd react in a very basic way.

The problem with this line of reasoning was that, prior to going to WIWE, he'd stopped by his departmental office at the university. While there, he'd been confronted with an *extremely* desirable female—a one-time seminar student of his who was, to put it bluntly, as buxom as she was brilliant.

Yet Meade had looked at her and felt nothing. Even after she'd made it abundantly clear that if he was interested, she was available, he hadn't experienced the faintest itch of attraction.

"Meade?" Brooke questioned a bit uncertainly. "Is something wrong?" The intensity of his gaze sent a peculiar shiver running through her body. He looked almost . . . angry.

"Wrong?" Meade repeated. He forked his fingers back through his hair in an abrupt, unthinking gesture, berating himself for his lack of self-control. "No. Everything's fine, Brooke. I'm just . . . just . . ." He shrugged, unable to come up with an acceptable explanation for his behavior. "It's nothing."

"Are you sure?" The skin between her brows pleated. She found herself wanting to . . . touch him. To soothe whatever was disturbing him. The urge was surprisingly strong, but she resisted it. Brooke had little faith in the power of her touch where men were concerned.

Meade managed a crooked smile. "Positive."

"Well, can I get you something?"

Maybe a bucket of ice to dump in my pants? he suggested silently.

"No, thank you," he said aloud. "Please, Brooke. Go take care of the flowers."

"All right," she acquiesced after a second or so. "Ah—why don't you sit down? I'll just be a minute."

She was actually three or four minutes, but Meade didn't object. He spent the first half of her absence lecturing his libido and the second half looking around her living room. It was done up with an airy, English country style he found very appealing. The color scheme—creams, golds, greens—was soft and soothing. A stone fireplace, somewhat smaller than his downstairs, was the focal point of the room. Most of the furniture was grouped around it.

The place was neat, as he'd expected it would be, given the way Brooke had taken care of his mail; yet it had a comfortable, lived-in feel. He sensed this was a home... not a temporary housing arrangement.

"Meade, these are so lovely—" Brooke said, coming back into the room. She'd arranged the flowers in a simple cylindrical glass vase, which she centered on the fireplace's mantel. "And the way they smell!" She buried her nose in the velvety petals of one blossom, inhaling the sweet but subtle perfume it exuded.

Meade found something very sensual about her appreciation of his gift. And he couldn't help but respond to that something. Feeling the renewed stirring of his body, he sought a safe topic.

"I like what you've done up here," he said, sitting down in one of the chintz-covered armchairs that flanked the fireplace.

Brooke turned toward him, smiling. "Thank you," she said. "But this was such a beautiful place to begin with—" She gestured with one hand. "I think I fell in love with it the second I walked in."

"So Daniel mentioned."

"Mr. Quincy?" Brooke stiffened slightly. "When did you talk to him?" Daniel Quincy had learned about Meade's early return from her that morning. He hadn't said anything—

"I stopped by WIWE a little after five," Meade responded, wondering about the hint of tension that had entered her posture. "I was hoping to catch you, but you'd already left. I ended up having a couple of welcome-home drinks with Daniel."

And Daniel, to Meade's frustration, had been a damned sight more generous with his private stock of single-malt whiskey than he'd been with his store of information about his executive assistant. About the only two nuggets he'd been able to pry out of the older man were that Brooke's marriage had lasted for six years and that she didn't seem to have much of a social life. But, aside from that—

Aside from that, Meade had had the strangest feeling that he'd learned more about Brooke Livingstone during their single encounter than Daniel Quincy had discovered about her in seven months.

"Oh . . . I see," Brooke responded slowly, moving to sit down on the sofa, which faced the fireplace. It was perfectly understandable, she told herself, that her name would come up in a conversation between her landlord and her employer. What did not make sense was Meade's explanation of why he'd gone to the institute in the first place. "You . . . you said you came to WIWE to see me—not Mr. Quincy?" she asked.

One corner of Meade's mouth turned up. "I wanted to ask you to have dinner with me."

Brooke's eyes widened and she felt a tinge of heat touch her cheeks. "Dinner—tonight?"

"Mmm, that was my original plan. Then Daniel told me you were already engaged. A, ah, command performance."

"Do you mean Amanda Wilding's party?" she inquired,

suppressing the impulse to laugh. The phrase "command performance" was extremely apt, but it really didn't do to mock the woman who had recently contributed one million dollars to WIWE!

"Exactly," Meade confirmed easily. He leaned forward. "Which brings me to the alternate to my original plan. Would you like an escort tonight?"

"An esc—Meade! You're going to *crash* Amanda Wilding's party?" Rumor had it that such a thing had been tried once in the past. However, it was unclear whether the uninvited guest had been struck by some form of divine retribution or merely arrested for breaking and entering.

Meade grinned roguishly, obviously amused by her shock. "What? And risk being hauled off to prison or turned into a pillar of salt?" he teased.

"Then, what—"

"I don't have to crash, Brooke. After I talked to Daniel, I called Amanda and told her I was back from the jungles of Brazil and looking for a good time."

"And she said—?" What he was telling her was utterly preposterous, of course. Yet, for reasons she couldn't begin to explain, Brooke suspected it was very close to the truth.

"Oh, she said she doubted her party was the place I was going to find the kind of good time I was looking for, but that I was welcome to drop by anyway."

Brooke gave a choke of laughter. "Are you serious?" she demanded.

Meade nodded, enjoying the sparkle dancing in her green eyes. "More or less. Look, I've been going to these soirées since I was an undergraduate. They're an anthropologist's dream. Pure tribal ritual. Besides, I genuinely like Amanda Wilding. Professor Browning introduced me to her. He used to say if she'd been born in another culture, she would have been a queen or a high priestess."

"I've also heard he once said if she'd been born in another century, she would have been burned at the stake as a witch."

"Yes, well, they had a mutual-admiration society that occasionally erupted into open warfare," Meade conceded wryly. "But, to get back to my alternate plan: Would you do me the honor of allowing me to escort you, tonight? You don't have to worry. Contrary to any impression I may've given you very early this morning, I *am* capable of civilized behavior."

"I—I don't understand," Brooke said after a moment, genuinely puzzled by his words. He'd spoken the last two sentences almost jokingly, yet she detected an underlying thread of seriousness.

"Well, the way you left my apartment—" he began.

Brooke felt a flash of alarm. Lord! She'd been so certain she'd hidden the turmoil she'd experienced after picking up that fertility figurine. *So certain.* After all, she'd put the thing down calmly and carefully instead of dropping it. And she'd waited a good five minutes before making her excuses and her exit, instead of bolting out of Meade's place and back to the relative safety of her own, as had been her original impulse.

"You think that was because of you?" she asked. That he'd been perceptive enough to pick up on her inner tumult, even if he'd misjudged the reasons for it, was more than a little unnerving.

Meade got up from his seat. He rubbed the back of his neck with his palm. "I have a tendency to go native when I'm in the field," he admitted after a few seconds. "Sometimes it takes me a while to get my party manners back in place." He looked over at her. "If I did anything . . . said anything . . ." Meade spread his hands.

Brooke shook her head. "No, no. It wasn't anything you did or said, Meade. Really." She paused, searching for a convincing explanation. She couldn't—wouldn't—tell him the truth. "I—I just suddenly realized I was very tired and needed to get some sleep," she went on. "I'm sorry if I seemed rude."

"You didn't." Meade wasn't sure *what* she'd seemed . . . or why. But he intended to find out.

Brooke rose, wanting to get off this topic. "Well, maybe it was a matter of the wine I was drinking going to my head," she suggested lightly, making a small adjustment in the hang of her dress.

Maybe, but Meade seriously doubted it. He'd seen her take four—perhaps five—sips of Chardonnay. Her glass had been half-full when she'd left.

"Are you sure there wasn't something I said or did that . . . upset you?" he persisted.

"Absolutely."

Meade searched Brooke's delicately featured face for another few seconds. She tilted her chin slightly, sustaining his gaze calmly.

One of the things Meade had learned in his unorthodox life had been when to push and when to be patient. Every instinct he had told him this was a time to be patient.

"Well, in that case," he said finally. "Would you like to go to Amanda Wilding's with me?"

"Yes," Brooke replied simply.

About ninety minutes later, Brooke was standing alone, studying the people moving around her. Meade had been right. It *was* pure tribal ritual.

She looked across the room to where Meade was engrossed in a conversation with Amanda Janaway Wilding. The silver-haired old woman had annexed him roughly twenty minutes before, her opening gambit a rather tart comment about his looking disappointingly well dressed for someone who'd spent eight months in the jungle. Meade had instantly responded with an outrageous apology about having sent all his loincloths to the cleaners'. After an obviously perfunctory cluck of protest, the formidable grande dame of Boston's formidable Wilding family had laughed out loud. Then, following several polite remarks to Brooke, she'd whisked Meade away.

A great many people, Brooke knew, found Amanda Wilding intimidating in the extreme. She herself had always felt a slight urge to drop a curtsy whenever the remarkable old woman made her imperious rounds at the institute. Meade, on the other hand . . . Well, she couldn't picture him being intimidated by *anybody.*

She could, however, picture him wearing a loincloth. Brooke could picture that with a vividness of detail that made the tips of her breasts harden against the lacy fabric of her bra.

Her fingers tightened around the slender crystal stem of the empty champagne glass she was holding. Taking a deep breath, she closed her eyes for a few moments, determinedly trying to banish—or at least blur—the powerful, primitive male image.

"So," said a faintly husky female voice from a few feet behind her. "What do you think about Meade O'Malley now that you've finally met him?"

Brooke's eyes popped open.

"Jazz!" she exclaimed, turning around to face the woman who, in the space of less than six months, had become a good friend. "What—I didn't expect to see you here tonight!"

Jazz O'Leary Wilding smiled back, her large gray eyes sparkling. "Well, expected or not, I'm here—and I'm impossible to overlook." She directed a mocking yet ineffably tender look downward at herself. She was *very* obviously pregnant.

For an instant, Brooke felt a familiar mix of emotions clutch at her heart and twist. Sadness . . . envy . . . anger. They were all there. There was happiness for Jazz, too, of course. Over the past months, she'd come to share in her friend's great joy. Yet, even in the midst of that sharing, there was the unanswerable question: *Why her and not me?*

"Is—is Ethan here, too?" she asked quickly, glancing around for the tall, distinguished-looking banker who was Jazz's husband. She didn't want Jazz to see what she feared her expression might betray. Her friend, Brooke had learned, was very sensitive to other people's pain.

Brooke had first been introduced to Ethan when he'd called on Daniel Quincy to finalize the arrangements surrounding Amanda Wilding's generous donation to the institute. During the course of a conversation, she'd made an offhand reference to where she was living. Ethan had responded that he knew the house, and its owner, Meade O'Malley, very well. One thing had led to another, and she'd ended up accepting an invitation to meet Ethan's wife.

Jazz shook her head, her red-gold tumble of curls bouncing. "Ethan's in California. When he isn't on the phone with me or my obstetrician, he's negotiating with the Japanese about a new investment consortium." The gamine features of her glowing face took on a mischievous cast. "Frankly, I'm glad he has something other than the baby to occupy him. I always thought I'd enjoy being waited on hand and foot, you know? But, honestly, Brooke, Ethan is being s-o-o-o solicitous, he's driving me crazy!"

"He's concerned about you, Jazz," Brooke said. "It's . . . natural."

"Well, I do love him for it," the redhead admitted, smoothing the turquoise silk of her maternity dress over her belly with gentle palms. "Still, I have to keep reminding him I'm tougher than I—ooh!" She caught her breath suddenly.

Brooke felt a pang of alarm. "Jazz?"

Jazz exhaled on what sounded like a laugh. "Ah . . . sorry," she apologized.

"Are you all right? I know the baby's due soon—"

"Two weeks. I'm—ah—okay, Brooke. I just get... it's nothing, really."

"Maybe you should sit down," Brooke suggested.

Jazz gave her a crooked smile. "Maybe that's a good idea," she agreed.

After discarding her champagne glass, Brooke ushered Jazz to an empty love seat in a relatively quiet corner of the room. Threading through the crowd was not easy. Neither was getting Jazz settled.

"Oh, God," Jazz lamented with mock despair. "I feel like a beached whale!" She adjusted her position gingerly.

"Is there anything I can do?" Brooke asked, seeing Jazz's face pale slightly. She sat down on the love seat, too.

"No... no," Jazz assured her. She inhaled through her nose, then exhaled slowly. "I've been having... I'm fine, really. So, ah, tell me. When did Meade get back?"

"Last night," Brooke answered automatically, still studying her friend's expression. "He flew in from—wait a minute! How did you know Meade was back?"

"I saw the two of you together when I waddled in a little while ago. I was going to come over to talk to you then, but Amanda waylaid me."

"Oh." Brooke's gaze involuntarily strayed toward the part of the room where she'd last seen Meade. She picked him out instantly. He was, to her, the most vivid person in the room.

Now that she'd had time to adjust to them, she realized that the changes in Meade were a matter of surface, not substance. Despite the new suavity of his dress and manner, there was still something very... elemental about him. He fit in, yet he stood apart. He seemed relaxed, yet Brooke had the sense he was ready for anything. His tall, athletic body radiated a coiled-spring alertness.

"Funny," Jazz mused. "I thought Meade was supposed to be gone until August."

"He was," Brooke answered, her eyes still fixed on the other side of the room. "But he finished his research project sooner than he expected." They'd talked a bit about what he'd been doing as they'd driven over. She'd found it fascinating.

"Mmmm. Well, Ethan's always said he had a reputation for being a fast worker."

Brooke gave Jazz a sharp look. "What's *that* supposed to mean?" she asked, coloring.

Jazz laughed. "Well . . . for one thing, he got his undergrad degree in three years." She tilted her head, her eyes dancing. "What did you *think* it was supposed to mean?" she inquired in dulcet tones.

Brooke toyed with her strand of pearls, feeling slightly embarrassed. "Nothing . . . nothing . . ."

"Uh-huh. Sure. Come on, Brooke. You've been listening to the legend of Boston's answer to Indiana Jones for months. Now that you've seen him in the flesh, what do you think?"

For one thing, Brooke thought she wished Jazz hadn't used the phrase "in the flesh."

When Meade found them ten minutes later, Brooke and Jazz were laughing together with what he could only describe as an air of feminine conspiracy. It reminded him of the huddling and giggling his twin sisters had done many years before.

"Well, well, well, Mrs. Wilding," he interrupted them, eyeing Jazz's midsection with undisguised interest. "I obviously don't need to ask what *you've* been doing for the last eight months."

"Meade!" Jazz exclaimed happily, looking up at him with a beaming smile. "I'd get up to give you a hello hug, but I'd need a crane to haul me out—"

"No problem." Meade leaned down to kiss her on both cheeks. While his friendship with Ethan Wilding dated back to his college years, his relationship with Ethan's wife was of much shorter standing. He nonetheless regarded Jazz with great affection and admiration. Straightening, he shook his head wonderingly. "My God, Jazz." His voice was gentle and, to Brooke's ears, held a trace of something close to awe. "You look—"

"Enormous? Humongous?" she supplied sassily. "Like I've been eating for twelve?"

Meade smiled. "I was going to say beautiful."

Although Jazz laughed and disputed this description, Brooke knew, with poignant certainty, that Meade O'Malley was telling the truth as he saw it.

Brooke later calculated that she, Jazz, and Meade spent about fifteen minutes talking before Jazz excused herself to use the powder room. Although she accepted Meade's help in getting to her feet, she shook her head to any additional assistance.

Almost simultaneously, a bearded, beetle-browed stranger with an exotic-sounding accent materialized and began embracing Meade as though he were his long-lost son. Based on Meade's rather restrained response to this exuberant greeting, Brooke gathered he regarded the bearded man in the nature of a distant cousin he'd just as soon have avoided seeing.

In the midst of Meade's reunion, Brooke herself was abruptly accosted by one of Daniel Quincy's numerous lady friends. The woman, it seemed, was writing a book and was just *dying* to ask some questions about preparing a manuscript for publication.

Eventually, the same social flow that tugged Brooke and Meade apart brought them back together.

"Here," Meade said with feeling, plucking two glasses of champagne off the polished silver tray being carried by a passing white-jacketed waiter. He handed one to Brooke. "You probably need this as much as I do."

Brooke smiled her thanks and sipped at the sparkling wine. She glanced around, noting that the crowd of guests had begun to thin. She wondered if Meade might be willing—?

Meade seemed to divine the direction of her thoughts. "I'm ready to get out of here if you are," he told her, taking a deep drink of his champagne.

"Do you read minds, Dr. O'Malley?" she inquired lightly.

"Only certain ones on certain subjects, Ms. Livingstone," he replied. He would have liked a little access to her thoughts about the handsome, old-school-tie type he'd spotted her conversing with a few minutes before. "Well?"

"I think leaving sounds like a wonderful idea," she told him frankly, then frowned as she remembered something. "Have you seen Jazz recently?"

Meade shook his head. "Not since she went off to the powder room."

"I haven't seen her since then, either."

"She probably decided to go home. She seemed a little . . . mmm . . . tired to me."

"I think she would have said good-bye to us before she went."

Meade frowned, then put down his champagne glass with a decisive clink. "There's one sure way to find out."

"Why, yes, Dr. O'Malley," Amanda Wilding's butler said. "I believe young Mrs. Wilding went into the study—oh, perhaps twenty minutes ago. She said something about needing to make a telephone call to California."

The door to the study was closed. Meade, his eyes on Brooke, rapped twice, then turned the ornate brass knob. "Jazz?" he questioned quietly as he pushed the door open.

Jazz was sitting at the massive mahogany desk, which was the dominant piece of furniture in the room. She was clutching a telephone receiver in one hand and holding the other one flat against her pregnant belly. She was as white as milk.

"I called Ethan to tell him he'd better get home because I'm pretty sure the baby's coming," she announced in a rather dazed voice. "But there's a terrible storm and the airport's closed and he's stuck in San Francisco."

Meade and Brooke exchanged glances and spoke simultaneously.

"Jazz—"

"Jazz—"

Jazz's gray eyes widened. "Help?" she pleaded.

"How . . . long?" Jazz asked.

Meade took the washcloth he'd just moistened in a bowl of cool water and used it to blot the perspiration that filmed Jazz's forehead. He was tempted to use the cloth on himself, too. He felt as though he'd sweated off ten pounds in the past seven and a half hours.

"A little more than two hours," he said reassuringly, glancing at the clock on the wall. It was nearing seven A.M. He breathed a silent prayer of thanks for the weather front that had finally cleared enough to allow Ethan Wilding's private jet to take off from San Francisco. His estimated time of arrival in Boston was five past nine. All signs pointed to his being by his wife's side when she delivered their first child.

"A little more than two hours?" Jazz repeated in a horrified tone, the pupils of her storm cloud–colored eyes dilating. "I—ah-ah—I've only been in labor a little more than *two hours*?!" Her voice rose on the last two words and her body seemed to go taut.

"No . . . no, Jazz," Brooke assured her soothingly, leaning over to stroke her friend's damp curls. "Meade thought you were asking how long until Ethan gets here."

"He . . . did?"

Brooke nodded, still stroking. "You're doing wonderfully, Jazz."

Jazz drew a shuddery breath, then released it in a hiccuppy laugh. "Oh . . . th-thank G-God," she said, relaxing visibly. Her eyelids fluttered shut for a moment.

Brooke felt Meade's eyes on her and looked questioningly across the bed at him. He gave her a warm smile and a tiny nod, then mouthed the word "thanks." She felt her lips curve upward in response to his nonverbal praise.

At the start, Brooke hadn't thought she'd be able to do what Jazz was asking of her. She'd changed into scrub clothes, done everything else the obstetrical staff had instructed her to do, and told herself she was ready. Yet, when she'd opened the door to the labor room Jazz had been placed in, she'd almost balked.

But *almost* wasn't the same as *actually*. Something—Brooke doubted she'd ever be sure what—had given her the strength to go in and offer whatever help she could.

Jazz groaned, then inhaled audibly through her nose.

"Good . . . good, Jazz," Meade encouraged. His voice, Brooke had noticed, had taken on a husky, near-hypnotic quality as the hours had slipped away. His tone was soothing, almost sensual, yet full of an elemental strength. "Go with the contraction . . . don't fight it. Good . . . good. I know this is rough, but you're doing fine, Jazz. Just fine. Okay . . . you're over the peak. Relax . . . relax. Let go of it. Breathe out the way you practiced . . . good."

Air came out of Jazz's mouth in an explosive rush. "That—that's another one down . . ." she panted. "Six-sixty j-jillion to go."

Meade chuckled. "No more than fifty-nine jillion, I promise."

"You're doing wonderfully, Jazz," Brooke said sincerely. She saw the pale-skinned redhead swallow and grimace. Immediately, she scooped up a small ice cube from a glass sitting on the bedside table next to her and put it between Jazz's lips. Jazz sucked it with a sigh.

"Mmmm . . ."

"Better?" Brooke asked softly.

"Mmmm . . ." Jazz nodded. She shifted a little. "Guh . . . good."

More than good, Meade thought, watching Brooke respond to each one of Jazz's unspoken needs. Much more.

He'd seen an emotion very close to panic on Brooke's face when she'd stepped into the labor room. For an instant, he'd thought she was suffering the same kind of nerves he was. Lord knew, he'd had a squadron of iron butterflies dive-bombing around in his belly when he'd contemplated what was ahead. But then he'd realized that his first impression was wrong. Whatever Brooke was afraid of, it ran far deeper, was far more personal, than any anxiety he was feeling.

He remembered opening his mouth to say something. Exactly what it had been, he wasn't certain now. He probably hadn't even been certain then. But, before he could get a word out, he'd seen Brooke's expression change as though, by sheer force of will, she'd banished her fears. She'd given him a calm nod and Jazz a comforting smile . . .

"Oh . . . gaaah—" Jazz seemed to be trying to suck all the air in the room inside her lungs when she inhaled this time.

"Good, good," Meade assured her immediately, deliberately dropping his voice to a low, even pitch. It was a technique he'd once observed a tribal shaman use to remarkable effect. Keeping his eyes locked on Jazz's face, he reached down to place his hand on her abdomen to massage it as the nurse who'd been in a little while earlier had suggested. But, instead of placing his palm directly against the taut curve of Jazz's belly, he found it covering Brooke's hand.

The feel of Meade's hand fitting over hers sent a shock

skittering all the way up Brooke's arm—from wrist to elbow to shoulder. She tightened her fingers for just an instant, then recovered. She started to stroke as she had intended to do, circling gently. Meade's hand stayed where it was,moving in uncanny harmony with hers, helping to ease Jazz through her current contraction.

And the next one.

And the next one . . .

After a time, Brooke lost all sense of where what she was doing stopped and what Meade was doing began. It seemed to her they were doing everything together.

"It . . . hurts!" Jazz protested, trying to catch her breath.

Brooke bit her lip and looked at the clock on the wall. It was 9:10 A.M. Meade had left the room a few minutes before. A nurse had come in as he was going out and attended to Jazz in briskly compassionate fashion. After informing her—and Brooke—that everything was going just as it should and that the doctor was expected shortly, she'd bustled out.

"You're doing fine, Jazz," Brooke said, trying to adopt a smooth, flowing tone like the one she'd been hearing Meade use for hours. "I know it's hard . . . I know it hurts. But, remember what the nurse said? The stronger the contractions, the sooner your baby will come."

"Not . . . be . . . fore . . . Ethan!"

"No, no. He's coming. He'll be here," Brooke said quickly, drawing the back of her hand across her forehead. She was starting to feel very weary and more than a little bit worried. It was obvious to her that Jazz's labor was becoming increasingly intense. It was also obvious to her that Jazz was becoming more and more restless and uncertain as the pain got worse.

At least the steady electronic bleep-bleep-bleep of the fetal monitor indicated a strong, healthy heartbeat. Early on, Brooke had found the sound a bit distracting. Now she took comfort in it.

Jazz grabbed hold of one of Brooke's hands and squeezed. "Oh . . . oh . . . oh . . ."

"Good . . . good . . ." Brooke responded, wincing inwardly at the convulsive strength of her friend's desperate grip.

"Af . . . raid!" Jazz panted. Her gray eyes were cloudy, not crystalline with anticipation the way they had been earlier.

"I know. I understand. But you shouldn't be afraid," Brooke said, using her free hand to squeeze out a washcloth and wipe the perspiration off Jazz's face and throat. "You're doing so well . . . so very well . . ." She wondered fleetingly if Meade had begun to feel like a broken record after repeating the same words of support over and over and over again.

"No." Jazz shook her head back and forth, her breath growing shallow. "After. Bad . . . muh—ther."

It took Brooke a moment to realize what Jazz meant. She felt a rush of emotion. Jazz had not confided a lot of details about her background, but what little she *had* said had painted a bleek picture of an unwanted, emotionally abused child who'd come of age hurting in a hundred different ways.

"No, no, Jazz," Brooke contradicted urgently.

Jazz's features contorted for a second. "May . . . ay . . . uhh . . . maybe!" she insisted.

"Jazz, no!" Brooke told her firmly, almost fiercely. She leaned over her friend, trying to establish eye contact. "You're going to have a beautiful baby and you're going to be a wonderful mother! Think of what a terrific job you've done with your kids—the ones at the juvenile counseling center. Think of it, Jazz. You take kids whose lives are in pieces and you help put them back together again. You love them. You teach them. I've seen how wonderful you are with them. And you'll be the same way with your baby. *Your baby.* The one you're working so hard for right n-now." She stopped for a second, realizing emotion and exhaustion had brought her close to tears. She swallowed hard. "You're going to be fine, Jazz. Fine . . ."

Jazz stared up at her. "Fine?" she asked weakly.

"Better than fine," Meade declared in a voice roughened by hours of nonstop talking. He'd returned just as Brooke had launched into her impassioned defense of Jazz's potentional as a mother. The depth of feeling he could hear in her words moved him in ways he couldn't begin to explain.

Jazz strained forward. "Ethan?"

Meade crossed quickly to the bed. "He's on the ground. He's on his way, Jazz. I think Amanda had a police escort waiting for him at the airport. Ethan's coming . . . just like the baby."

"Just like the baby," Brooke echoed.

The next time the door to the labor room opened it was to admit Ethan Wilding, a doctor, and two nurses.

Jazz, at the peak of a contraction, sobbed out her husband's name.

Brooke watched as Ethan Wilding crossed to his wife. She heard him say Jazz's name once, twice, three times. She saw him touch Jazz's cheek.

And suddenly, Brooke realized that there was no need for her or Meade . . . not in this place. Not anymore.

A strong male arm curved supportively around her shoulders. After a moment, she shifted and looked up into Archimedes Xavier O'Malley's face.

He still looked like a walk-the-plank pirate, Brooke thought, examining the compelling planes and hollows of his striking features. But a Greek god? No. The emotions she read in Meade's deep blue eyes made it clear he was very, very human.

She felt the hard muscles of his arm tense and his fingers tighten against her flesh. He drew her close against him.

"Meade?" she asked.

"I don't think anyone would miss us if we left," he said simply.

Chapter 3

BROOKE DIDN'T REALIZE SHE'D STARTED crying until Meade told her.

"It's all right, Brooke," he assured her quietly, stroking away the tear that was trickling down her pale cheek with the pad of his thumb. He felt her tremble at the contact. The green eyes that gazed up at him were clouded and more than a little confused.

"Wh-what?" Brooke asked, uncertain of why he'd touched her. The hospital corridor they were standing in was brightly lit and bustling with activity. Stepping out into it from the labor room had disoriented her, leaving her feeling woozy. She was having trouble focusing. One second everything was crystal clear; the next second everything was blurred. It was as though she were in the middle of a pretentious, badly shot art film.

"You're crying, sweetheart," Meade told her, gently brushing away another tear. Her skin was very soft against his fingertips.

His casual use of the endearment caught Brooke by surprise. For a moment, the sense of his first two words got lost in the pleasurable shock of his third. Then, abruptly, her brain registered what he'd said. Brooke lifted a hand to her face. She *was* crying. Her cheeks were damp with tears she hadn't been aware of shedding.

"I—I'm sorry," she stammered, blinking and swallowing hard. She wiped both sides of her face and gave an inelegant sniff. "I—I didn't know—"

"It's all right, Brooke," Meade said. "I understand."

"I don't usually—" she started, wanting to explain. Crying in public was not something she made a practice of. "I mean, I can't—" She knuckled beneath her eyes, trying to sort out the unsettling combination of emotions that was rioting through her. "Everything is—is—" She averted her face for a second, feeling extraordinarily vulnerable.

Meade hooked two fingers beneath Brooke's chin and made her look at him. His blue eyes had darkened to the color of a clear midnight sky. In the vivid depths of them, Brooke saw echoes of what she was feeling. The powerful sense of connection she'd experienced in the labor room came back in full force.

"I understand," Meade said, withdrawing his hand. His voice was a bit husky. "Believe me, Brooke, I really do understand. What we just went through was . . ." He paused, searching for a way to describe the hours they'd shared since Jazz had made her plea for help in Amanda Wilding's study.

Exhilarating? Exhausting? Unforgettable? Unique? Each word defined a part of the experience, but not the whole.

"It was . . . overwhelming," he concluded, acknowledging the essential inadequacy of the adjective with a crooked smile even as he said it.

Brooke gave a watery little chuckle. "Overwhelming," she agreed, then answered his smile with one of her own. "I feel like . . . like . . ." she gestured, palms up, then admitted: "I don't know *what* I feel like!"

Meade laughed low in his throat. "I, personally, feel

like about twelve hours of sleep," he said. He also felt like pulling Brooke into his arms and kissing her to seal the almost tangible bond he now felt with her, but he resisted the impulse.

No, he told himself. *Not yet. But soon. Very soon.*

"Sleep?" Brooke challenged lightly, giving her cheeks one last brush with her fingers. Her tears had dried. "Are you tired?"

"Oh, just a little," Meade returned wryly, glancing toward the labor room door. He saw Brooke's eyes move in the same direction. "I know we actually had the easy part tonight," he commented. "But, still—"

"Still?"

He grinned. "It's the old joke. The reason they call it labor is because it's so damned much work!"

It *was* an old joke, and it *wasn't* really that funny, but Brooke started to laugh at it anyway. After a moment, Meade did, too. Hearing the sound of his laughter did something to Brooke. She suddenly felt as light as a bubble. If someone had informed her that the hospital corridor had just been pumped full of giggle gas, she wouldn't have doubted it for a moment.

Her giddiness was such that she almost lost her balance and stumbled into the path of an oncoming food-tray wagon. Meade, who registered the danger and responded to it in a purely reflexive manner, managed to jerk her out of the way in the nick of time. The gawky young man who was pushing the battered metal kitchen cart rolled his eyes as though wondering what two escapees from the psychiatric ward were doing loose in the obstetrical unit, but he didn't break stride. He simply kept going.

For some crazy reason, the realization that she had just narrowly escaped ending up splat on the floor with treadmarks running down her spine struck Brooke as incredibly funny. Although she did her best to say a few coherent words of thanks to her rescuer, she was laughing too hard to make much sense. Concerned about the possibility of disturbing patients, she pressed one palm over her mouth, trying to bottle up the giggles bubbling out of her throat. A quick glance in Meade's direction told her that his self-control was only marginally better than hers.

Finally, like a child's wind-up toy, Brooke's irresistible attack of hilarity began to run down. She slumped against the corridor wall for support. Meade did the same.

"Oh . . . my . . ." she gasped, trying to smooth out her disordered breathing pattern.

"Right," Meade concurred with feeling, raking his fingers back through his hair.

He wondered if he might be suffering from oxygen deprivation. He remembered experiencing this type of light-headedness only once before. It had happened the first time he'd traveled to Mexico City with Professor Browning. He'd been warned about the altitude, of course. But, at barely sixteen, he'd been afflicted with a typically adolescent belief in his immunity to all the physical weaknesses that affected other people. Unfortunately for him, his belief had been wrong.

Meade sucked in a deep breath, filling his lungs with air. He exhaled slowly. He repeated the process several times, eventually feeling the jumping-bean hop of his pulse return to normal.

From high human drama to hysterical laughter in ten hours. What a trip! he thought, turning his head toward Brooke. *And what a woman to make it with . . .*

Brooke felt the caress of Meade's gaze and looked over at him. The expression in his sky-colored eyes made her last, lingering impulse to laugh melt away like a snowflake in summer sunshine.

"You were wonderful in there with Jazz, you know," Meade said, his voice low and resonant.

"M-me?" A mixture of surprise and pleasure stained Brooke's cheeks a hot rose. Then, recovering a little, she shook her head. The movement loosened her already-coming-unpinned hair, and a lock of it tumbled down over her brow. She batted it away. "No. *You're* the one who was wonderful, Meade! The way you helped Jazz. The way you found just the right words to encourage her. It was so . . . so . . . Jazz couldn't have—I mean, what you did—"

Meade reached over and silenced Brooke's disjointed but deeply felt outpouring by pressing two fingers against her lips for a brief moment. "What *we* did," he corrected. "It was the two of us, Brooke. The two of us—together."

Fleeting though the contact had been, Meade's touch still sent a star shower of pleasure cascading through Brooke's body. In another place, at another time, she might have been afraid of the sensations he evoked in her—afraid those sensations made promises that would never—*could* never—be fulfilled. But here, now, after what they'd been through, she simply savored what she was feeling. Anything promised seemed possible at this moment . . . with this man.

"Together . . ." she repeated, cherishing the word as she might a special gift. "We—we made a good team, didn't we?" She brushed at her hair again.

Meade smiled. "We made a *terrific* team."

One corner of Brooke's mouth turned up. "All right," she conceded. "A *terrific* team." She paused, growing reflective. The memory of the emotional moments she'd witnessed right after Ethan Wilding had made his entrance into the labor room filled her mind. So much love between a man and a woman, she thought. Ethan and Jazz had what she'd always hoped for . . . dreamed of . . .

"Brooke?" Meade questioned, seeing the wistfulness that had settled across her face like a shadowy lace veil. "What is it?"

Brooke gave a small sigh. "I was just thinking about Jazz and Ethan," she said. "I'm so glad he got here in time. When he came into the labor room . . . the way he looked

. . . it was . . . was . . ." She let her voice trail off. Some things simply could not be put into words.

"I know. I saw," Meade answered. "Having the chance to be with the woman you love as she gives birth to the new life you've created together . . ." He shook his head wonderingly. "It must be like nothing else in the world."

Brooke heard a yearning—something akin to envy—in his voice. She understood all too well the longing he obviously felt.

She looked away as she felt the warning prick of tears. Tilting her head back, she closed her eyes for a few seconds. She was *not* going to start crying again!

"Tired?" Meade asked, studying her profile. The wistfulness in her features had given way to a hint of strain.

Steeling herself, Brooke opened her eyes and met his questioning gaze. "A little," she conceded.

"Well, then, maybe we should think about heading home—again."

"Again—?" Brooke began, slightly puzzled. Then she realized what Meade meant. They'd been "heading home" when they'd found Jazz. "Oh—yes. Maybe we should." She spoke with a curious sense of reluctance.

Meade looked down at the loose-fitting green scrub outfit he'd donned what now seemed like a lifetime ago. The cotton garments were badly rumpled. The short-sleeved top bore several perspiration stains. "Do you have any idea where our real clothes are?" he inquired.

"Ah . . . I think mine may be in the nurses' locker room," Brooke replied slowly, trying to recall exactly what she'd done with her things when she'd changed. "But I'm not—" she broke off, suddenly realizing the source of the reluctance she'd been conscious of a moment before. She put her hand on Meade's forearm. "Do you really want to go home?" she asked.

Meade remained silent for a few seconds, caught by the

urgency of her inflection and the feel of her fingers on his flesh. "Don't you?"

"No," Brooke said simply. "No, I don't. Not yet. Not when—" she glanced over her shoulder toward the labor room where Jazz was. "I'd like to stay until Jazz's baby is born, Meade. Does that . . . does that sound crazy to you?"

Meade's lips curved up slowly. He covered Brooke's hand with his and gave her fingers a gentle squeeze. "No, it doesn't sound crazy at all," he told her frankly. "What do you say we find somewhere to sit down while we wait?"

By mutual agreement, they decided to avoid the area set aside for expectant fathers. So, the "somewhere to sit down" ended up being a mulch-brown couch in a small alcove across from the nurses' station. The couch was as uncomfortable as it was ugly, but Brooke didn't mind. She was so grateful to get off her feet, she barely noticed the fact that the cushion she more or less collapsed onto sagged beneath her weight like a cheap hammock.

"Ahh . . ." she sighed, leaning back.

Meade sat down next to her. His cushion gave an almost-human-sounding groan and he suddenly felt himself sinking into a craterlike depression. The lap of luxury it wasn't; but that didn't trouble Meade in the least. Luxury had never been a particularly high priority with him. Besides, as unaccommodating as this particular piece of furniture was, it was a damned sight more pleasant to sit on than a lot of things he could think of!

Meade shifted, settling himself, then stretched out his legs. He took a long, deep breath and expelled it through his nostrils.

"Oh, no!" Brooke exclaimed abruptly. She sat bolt upright, her eyes wide with alarm. "Ohmigod!"

Meade stiffened. "What?"

She gave him an appalled look. "I completely forgot!

I'm supposed to be at work, Meade. Mr. Quincy will be wondering—"

"No, he won't," Meade interrupted, shaking his head. "The last time I went out of the labor room to check on where Ethan was, I gave Daniel a call. Since he left the party before all the excitement with Jazz started, I thought he'd appreciate knowing what was going on. He said to tell you you've got the day off."

"Oh . . ." Brooke took a moment to digest this. "Ah—thank you."

"You're welcome." He massaged the back of his neck with one hand, willing the tension out of his body.

Brooke leaned back against the couch once more. "Do you think we should call Amanda Wilding?"

"Not necessary," Meade answered dryly. "One of the nurses told me the chief of obstetrics himself has been keeping her up-to-date."

Brooke lifted her brows. "Impressive."

"Predictable, when you consider the newest addition to this hospital is called the Wilding Wing."

"True," Brooke nodded.

There was a brief silence then. Brooke looked around. The alcove was empty except for the two of them, but several half-empty containers of coffee and an ashtray filled with cigarette butts spoke of other visitors . . . other vigils.

"Do you think it will be long?" she asked Meade.

"What? Before Jazz has her baby?"

"Yes."

"Mmm . . ." Meade rubbed his jaw. New whisker growth rasped his fingers like sandpaper. "Well, I'm certainly not an expert, but I think she was going into transition when Ethan got there. That's supposed to be the roughest part of labor, but it doesn't usually last long. So

. . . maybe an hour. An hour and a half. Of course, since this is Jazz's first . . ."

"For someone who's not an expert, you sound pretty knowledgeable," Brooke commented.

Meade shrugged. "Osmosis."

"What?"

"My two sisters—Kathleen and Mary Margaret—have five kids between them. I've heard a lot about the, ah, ins and outs of labor."

"Oh." Judging by the way he'd been with Jazz, Brooke thought, he'd obviously learned from what he'd heard.

"Aside from that, my main claim to obstetrical experience is having seen a baby delivered two weeks after my nineteenth birthday." His mouth twisted, indicating his feelings about this episode were rather mixed.

"Really?" This was one Archimedes O'Malley exploit Brooke hadn't heard about. "How—what happened?"

"Well, it was in this backwater village in Panama. I was part of an expedition Professor Browning put together to cross the Darién Gap. That's a couple of hundred miles of rain forest and swamp in the northwestern corner of the country. Not exactly paradise on earth. Anyway, we were all sitting in this tiny cantina one night making bets about what was in the stew we were eating when a Kuna Indian woman came stumbling in and collapsed on the floor, clutching her belly and moaning. The cantina owner was all for heaving her out, but the professor stopped him with a fistful of cash. Then he coolly announced that since the woman was obviously in labor and since there didn't seem to be a doctor in the house, we were going to have to help her."

"Which . . . you did?"

"Mmm, it was mainly a matter of letting nature take its course. Thank God the woman knew what she was supposed to do. We found out later she'd already had four children. Professor Browning had read enough medical textbooks to have some idea of what was going on. As for the rest of the team—well, one guy, the Mr. Macho of our crew, keeled over in a dead faint. Two others got busy boiling water. Why, I have no idea. As for me—"

"Yes?" Brooke prompted. "What did you do?"

"Well, I probably would have bolted out of the place if the woman hadn't grabbed on to my hand like it was a winning lottery ticket," Meade confessed with a rueful, self-deprecating chuckle. "What a grip! I ended up with a ringside seat at the delivery of a bouncing baby girl who came into the world, took one deep breath, and started screaming like a banshee." He shook his head. "It definitely made me think about what it meant to have a child."

"I . . . I can imagine."

Meade stretched. The cushion gave another groan. "So, what about you?"

For one awful instant, Brooke thought he was asking her thoughts about what it meant to have a child. "What about me?"

Meade stifled a yawn. "Have you ever helped deliver a baby?"

"Oh—oh, no." She shook her head quickly. "No. Never."

Her tone made Meade look at her very closely. He remembered the panic he'd seen on her face as she'd stood in the doorway of the labor room. There was an echo of that emotion flickering in her eyes now. Plainly, something about childbirth upset her.

"Well, no one ever would have guessed this was your first time," he told her softly, wanting to soothe even as he pondered the possible sources of her fear. "As I said before, you were wonderful."

* * *

Their conversation drifted casually after that, eventually dwindling into companionable silence. Brooke yawned, feeling the tension ease out of her body. For reasons she couldn't explain and didn't particularly want to explore, the couch had begun to seem quite . . . comfortable . . .

Meade was half-asleep when Brooke's head dropped heavily against his shoulder. While his body jerked to instant alert, his brain lagged a second or so behind. He experienced a momentary uncertainty about where he was, how he'd gotten there, and whom he was with. Then full awareness kicked in.

"Hmmnmn-uhn," Brooke mumbled, shifting. "Hunhh-hmm."

"Brooke?" Meade asked.

She shifted again. The contact between her body and his increased. So did his pulse rate. Muttering under her breath, Brooke squirmed around like a kitten in a basket. Meade felt her breasts brush against his arm.

"Brooke?" he repeated. His voice was softer than the first time he'd said her name, but had a hint of urgency to it.

Brooke's shifting and squirming turned into something very close to snuggling. She murmured several syllables that made absolutely no sense, yet still sounded remarkably like an invitation. Again, Meade felt the soft weight of her breasts against his upper arm. The tips of them were beginning to harden. She turned her head, and her hair spilled across his throat, tickling the underside of his jaw.

Meade groaned through gritted teeth, embarrassingly aware of the hardening of his own body. Desire massaged his groin like a heated velvet hand. If Brooke had this effect on him when she was *asleep*—!

"Mmm . . ." Brooke sighed, apparently finding a position that pleased her. The restless, unconsciously arousing movements of her body slacked off and she went as pliant as melting wax. "Mmmm . . ."

Meade forced himself to take a long breath and expel it very slowly. Then he forced himself to take *another* long breath and expel *it* very, *very* slowly. He concentrated on the feel of the air filling and leaving his lungs. Keep your mind above your belt, he ordered himself.

After a few minutes of determinedly redirecting his physical impulses, Meade put an arm around Brooke and carefully eased her into a less provocative position. She made a contented little sound deep in her throat and nodded her head. The tangled silk of her hair fell forward, veiling her face.

Meade pushed the hair back with a gentle, combing stroke, sifting the fine strands through his fingers. He gazed down at Brooke. He could see the movement of her eyes beneath the fragile skin of her lids and wondered what she was dreaming about. A faint tinge of pink stole across her cheeks. Her lips parted for an instant to reveal the tip of her tongue.

Lord, she was lovely! She was lovely, and Meade wanted her very much. But not just physically. His need for her went beyond sexual hunger . . .

His mind flashed back to the music he'd been playing —could it really have been only two days ago? The music that, in a sense, had brought Brooke Livingstone to him. "Melodies to Mate By," according to the irreverent enthno-musicologist who'd given him the tape.

Melodies to Mate By. In truth, the music of courtship rituals and marriage ceremonies.

Meade closed his eyes. Courtship? Marriage?

He thought of what Sebastian and Gabrielle Browning had had. Of what his parents, Francis and Eleni, still had.

Courtship . . . marriage . . . children?

He thought of Ethan and Jazz Wilding.

Meade opened his eyes and looked down at Brooke

once again. He was still looking at her when sleep claimed him.

The sound of a throat being cleared brought Meade awake. Two facts imposed themselves on his brain simultaneously. Number One: His dream of holding a serenely sleeping Brooke Livingstone encircled in his arms was no dream. And, Number Two: Ethan Wilding was standing about a foot away wearing the broadest grin he'd ever seen.

"Eth-Ethan!" Meade exclaimed.

Is there an earthquake? Brooke asked herself fuzzily, wondering why the wonderfully warm and comfortable pillow beneath her cheek was suddenly moving around as though it had come ali—

Brooke's eyes flew open. The realization of where she was and who she was with was as rousing as a slap with a cold washcloth.

"Meade, what—?" she started, struggling to sit up. Her hair tumbled into her eyes and she swatted it out of the way with a hiss of impatience. As she did so, she registered the presence of a third person. "E-Ethan!"

"That's my name," Ethan acknowledged wryly. He was more disheveled than Brooke had ever seen him, but his Bostonian poise seemed very much intact.

Meade rose to his feet with something less than his usual feline grace. "Jazz?" he asked.

"Mother and son are doing fine," Ethan reported with unmistakable pride.

"Jazz—Jazz had a boy?" Brooke questioned, making a few tugging adjustments to her clothes as she, too, got up from the couch. The embarrassment she normally would have felt at having been discovered asleep in the arms of a man she'd known for less than two days was lost in her excitement at Ethan's news.

"Seven pounds, six ounces," came the announcement.

"And he's got his mother's red hair. He looks like someone spread marmalade all over his skull."

"Congratulations, Ethan," Meade said warmly, extending his hand to his friend.

"Thank you," Ethan responded as he and Meade shook. "For a lot more than your kind words . . ." He turned to Brooke. "And thank you, too, Brooke."

"I'm so happy for you and Jazz," she told him sincerely.

"I appreciate hearing that." Ethan paused for a moment, looking back and forth between Meade and Brooke. "What you both did for Jazz . . ." he began slowly, obviously struggling to find the best way to express his feelings. "It was—I really don't know how to tell you—"

"No speeches necessary, Ethan," Meade interrupted. He glanced over at Brooke. "We're glad we could help."

"Yes," she agreed, meeting Meade's eyes and smiling. "Yes . . . we are. Very glad."

There was a pause then, as though words weren't necessary. It was punctuated by a tremendous yawn from Meade. An instant later, Brooke yawned as well.

"Long night?" Ethan asked with just a hint of humor.

Meade chuckled briefly. "You might say that." Then, because it struck him as the most natural thing in the world to do, he slipped an arm around Brooke. "Is there any chance of us getting to see the new mother?"

"Mmmm." Ethan shook his head regretfully. "She's asleep right now, Meade. It was . . . a long night for her, too."

"What about the—ahhh—baby?" Brooke asked, covering her mouth with her hand as she tried to swallow another yawn. Without really thinking about it, she leaned her head against Meade's shoulder.

"He's in the room with Jazz. And he was sound asleep, too, when I left."

"Well, then, we'll just have to come back," Meade said philosophically. "Have you decided on a name yet?"

Ethan smiled. "It's under negotiation," he joked, then grew serious. "Look, I really want to—there must be *something* I can do for you two. Please. Anything. Anything at all."

Brooke and Meade traded glances.

"Coffee would be nice," he commented after a moment.

"And you could help find our clothes," she added.

"We could use a car, too. Amanda had her driver bring us to the hospital, but he's long gone."

"Coffee . . . clothes . . . and a car," Ethan repeated. "I think that can be arranged."

About an hour later, Brooke Livingstone stood at the foot of the stairs in the entrance foyer of Archimedes Xavier O'Malley's house, looking up at her landlord with a sleepy smile.

"I don't know why you told Ethan he and Jazz shouldn't feel obligated to name the baby after us," she said reflectively. "I think Livingstone Archimedes Wilding has a very . . . mmm . . . distinguished ring to it."

"Not quite as distinguished as Archimedes Livingstone," Meade retorted. The foyer was bathed in the honeyed glow of early afternoon sunshine. He found himself admiring the way the light shimmered through Brooke's hair . . . envying the way it caressed and warmed her skin. "But, either way, the poor kid would probably be in high school before he learned to spell his whole name."

"We-l-l-l . . . I suppose you have a point." Brooke leaned against the beautifully carved newel post behind her, toying with the strand of pearls at her throat. She knew she should go up to her apartment, but she couldn't make herself. Not just yet.

Something was happening to her. No. Something *had* happened to her. And it had started with the music . . .

What Brooke did next, she'd wanted to do since the first time she'd seen Meade. She lifted one hand and touched his face. She brushed her fingertips down the strong line of his cheek and jaw, learning the unyielding feel of the bone beneath the resilient flesh. She saw his eyes darken and experienced a quiver of expectation.

Meade caught her hand in his and turned it over. Dipping his head, he pressed his lips against the center of her palm. He heard her breath catch.

"Why—?" she whispered. She wasn't certain whether she was asking *why me*, *why you* or *why now.*

"I don't know," Meade said almost harshly, then pulled her into his arms.

He sensed a heartbeat's worth of hesitation before Brooke's slender body yielded against his. It was very brief, but it was there. Yet, before he had a chance to stop and question it, Brooke rose on tiptoe and offered him her mouth.

Meade took what was offered, slanting his head slightly, claiming her lips with his. He brought one hand up, charting the supple line of Brooke's spine, finding the place where the fine-textured fabric of her yellow dress gave way to the even finer feel of her naked skin. He stroked through the loose tendrils at her nape, then tangled his fingers deep in her hair.

Ribbons of pleasure spread through Brooke's body, twisting themselves around her nerves and twining into her most sensitive places. Hunger hummed within her. Emboldened by unfamiliar yet irresistible appetites, she let her hands wander, sliding them up Meade's arms to his broad shoulders. She felt the ripple of his muscles through the fabric of his clothing. She shifted her hips in an involuntary movement and heard Meade make a noise deep in his chest.

She realized what she had done. What she wanted to go on doing. The realization made her tremble.

She could . . . she couldn't . . . she could . . .

Meade teased at Brooke's mouth with the tip of his

tongue, seeking a deeper and more intimate access. He experienced a flash of surprise and a bit of frustration when her lips did not part beneath the coaxing courtship.

The probe of Meade's tongue was as skilled as it was sensual. Brooke felt echoes of the seductive stroking reverberate throughout her body. The sensations were erotic, yet vaguely alarming in their potency.

She couldn't . . . she could . . .

If she didn't, she'd displease him. But, if she did—

You want to know why, Brooke? Peter had mocked when she'd asked him the reason for his infidelity. *Because I'm a man and I can't get what I want—what I need—from you! You can't give me a son and you can't give me much satisfaction, either! You're not just infertile—you're frigid, too!*

Acquired reluctance opened war on instinctive response and, in the end, acquired reluctance won. The lessons of her marriage had been humiliating and painful; but Brooke had learned them very, very well.

She couldn't.

Meade felt Brooke stiffen and start to pull away from him. He fought down an almost savage desire to hold on to her. He knew, with absolute certainty, that he was capable of overcoming her sudden resistance—whatever its source.

He also knew that to do so he would have to make one of the biggest mistakes of his life.

Meade let Brooke go. Then he took a step back from her.

Trembling, Brooke bit her lip. She knotted and unknotted her fingers. She didn't know whether she'd just been released or rejected. She searched Meade's face for signs of anger or contempt. She found only undisguised desire and unanswered questions. Many, many questions.

"I . . . I'm sorry, Meade," she said after a few seconds. "But—I've only known you—this is . . . this is happening too fast for me. Much too fast." She braced herself for Meade's reaction. In the back of her mind, she could hear the venomous words Peter had thrown at her the few times she'd refused his advances. They'd been almost as cruel as the ones he'd used when she'd tried to give him what he wanted—needed—and failed.

Meade heard the distress in her voice and saw the almost desperate expression in her wide green eyes. She was afraid. But of what? Him? Herself? The two of them together?

Of course, maybe a part of him was afraid as well. Of her. Of himself. Of the two of them together.

Meade smiled crookedly and traced the curve of Brooke's cheek with infinite care. "I haven't known you any longer than you've known me, sweetheart," he told her. "So, if this is happening too fast for you . . . well, we'll just have to go slower."

Chapter 4

THE WEEK THAT FOLLOWED THE kiss in the foyer was the oddest of Brooke's life.

The seven days, taken separately and together, had a kaleidoscopic quality. Always changing, endlessly fascinating. Each time Brooke thought she was starting to understand what was going on, something shifted and everything seemed new and different.

She saw Meade frequently during the week. At the house. At the institute. They had lunch together once, dinner twice. And, at her impulsive suggestion, they spent a Saturday afternoon wandering through the Arnold Arboretum.

Their encounters were far more friendly than flirtatious. Brooke greatly enjoyed Meade's company and sensed he felt the same about hers. They disagreed about a lot of things, but agreed about a great many more. They had similar senses of humor and found much to laugh about.

Yet, through every waking moment, Brooke had been conscious of an undercurrent of electricity . . . of expectation. A casual brushing of their fingers—never more than that!—and her heart would be racing like the favorite in the Kentucky Derby. A brief meeting of their eyes and her pulse would start to pound. Even when she wasn't with Meade . . .

At the end of the oddest week of her life, Brooke arrived home from work to find Archimedes Xavier O'Malley in her bedroom.

She heard a pair of voices coming from the open door of her apartment as she climbed the stairs. She felt an odd little frisson of excitement dance up her spine as she identified one of the voices as Meade's. The other was unknown to her. It sounded like that of an older man and was flavored with the barest hint of an Irish lilt.

"—not trying to tell you what to do," the second voice was saying impatiently. "Lord knows, your mother and I have always believed in letting you go your own way, even when that way took you places we can't even find on the map! But we'd still like to see you settled, boy. Your mother and I aren't getting—"

"Any younger," Meade said. Brooke thought she heard equal parts of affection and exasperation in his tone. "I know. You've managed to work Social Security and senior citizens discounts into the conversation at least six times already. But, I have to tell you, Pop. This declining-years routine of yours would be a lot more believable if you hadn't mentioned that Mother's decided to take karate lessons along with her aerobics class and that you're thinking of buying a motorcycle."

"Dammit!" This pungent exclamation was followed by what sounded like a reluctant snort of laughter. "All right, so your mother and I aren't ready to move into some retirement village in Florida. That doesn't change the fact that you should have a family."

"I do."

"Of your own!"

By now, Brooke had nearly reached the doorway of her bedroom. She was feeling extremely uncomfortable about what she was overhearing. She hesitated for a moment; then, reminding herself that this *was* her apartment, she took the last step and looked in.

What she saw was Meade and a burly older man hunkered down on the floor, working on her air-conditioning unit. Whether they were in the process of dismantling it or putting it together, she couldn't tell. But it seemed obvious from the deftness of their movements that they knew what they were doing.

Meade, who was wearing wash-faded jeans and nothing else, had his back partially turned toward the door. The late-afternoon sunlight streaming in through the window where the air conditioner had been emphasized the smooth play of the taut muscles of his upper body. The red-and-black tattoo on his left shoulder blade looked even more exotic than it had the first time Brooke saw it.

"One of these days," Meade said calmly, reaching for a screwdriver. "There are some things you don't want to rush. Some things you have to take slowly. Give me awhile to—"

"Give you awhile, my Aunt Bonnie's best brass spittoon. I want grandchildren!" came the bracing reply. "Hand me that bolt, will you? Thank you. Just a few more minutes and we'll have this thing purring cool air like a kitten in the refrigerator."

"You've already got five grandchildren."

"Yes, and I love every blessed one of them dearly. Especially that eight-year-old rascal, Kevin. But they're Morellis and Cunninghams. Not O'Malleys. A man wants to know his name is going to live on after him."

"Well, if it comes down to that—" Meade broke off suddenly, as though sensing Brooke's presence. He glanced over his shoulder, then rose in a single, seamless movement. "Brooke!" he greeted her with a grin. His eyes ran over her appreciatively.

"Ah—hello, Meade," she returned, resisting the urge to pat her hair or adjust her skirt. "You—you're fixing my air conditioner?"

"When you asked me to recommend a repair service this morning I said I'd get somebody in to take care of it, remember?"

"Oh . . . yes." She'd bumped into Meade as she'd been leaving for work. He'd been coming in from what she'd assumed, judging by the perspiration-drenched state of his skimpy shorts and cutoff shirt, had been a long, hard run. The sight of his sweat-slick body had made her think of her broken air conditioner . . . and several other things. "But I didn't realize *you* were going to—"

"Do it yourself, get it done right," the older man said, wiping his hands on his trousers as he got to his feet. "Have me help, get it done better—and for free. I'm Francis O'Malley, young Meade's father."

"How do you do, Mr. O'Malley," Brooke responded politely. She didn't see many physical similarities between the two men. Francis O'Malley was quite a few inches shorter than his son and built as solid as an oak tree. He had short-cropped, steel gray hair that she was willing to bet had once been a blazing red. His eyes were a slate blue-gray and held an assessing glint. Brooke extended her hand to him. "I'm Brooke Livingstone, your son's tenant."

"Pleased to meet you," Meade's father returned, clasping her fingers as though they were made of exquisitely fragile bone china. "And, in case you're worrying, we know what we're doing here. I've had more than thirty-five years' experience as an electrician."

"Yes, I—I know." Brooke nodded. "Meade told me you were an electrical contractor."

"Ah." Francis O'Malley's brows rose in obviously pleased surprise. "Then you've been discussing families already, have you? Good. Good. So, now, tell me a little about yourself . . ."

"Meade," Brooke said firmly. "I didn't mind all your father's questions. Really, I didn't."

"I'm glad one of us didn't," Meade replied, taking a deep swallow of beer. It was about eight-thirty, and they were sitting in a booth in a neighborhood pizza place sharing a pepperoni, mushroom, and double-cheese pizza. They'd been there once before, early in the evening of the day Jazz and Ethan's baby had been born. "Sherlock O'Holmes at his worst."

"He was very charming," Brooke countered. She wasn't trying to make Meade feel better; she was telling the truth. Yes, Francis O'Malley had been one of the most inquisitive men she'd ever met. Yet he'd been so likable and so unabashedly interested in knowing who she was and what she had to say, that she hadn't been offended by his inquiries. In fact, she'd been surprisingly flattered by them.

"Charming? And I suppose you'd classify an interrogation by the Spanish Inquisition as a pleasant way to pass an afternoon?"

"Meade!"

He sighed, fishing a chunk of pepperoni off the pizza and popping it in his mouth. "I'm sorry," he apologized. "I love my father. He's one of the kindest, most generous men in the world. But, sometimes—God! There are moments when he—and my mother—share a one-track mind."

"You mean, they're . . . pushing you to get married and have a family."

"Oh, you picked up on that, did you?"

"Well, actually, I more or less heard your father say it as I was coming up the stairs," Brooke confessed. She lifted a slice of pizza to her mouth and nibbled a few bites.

An odd look passed over Meade's face, as though he

might be trying to remember exactly what he and his father had said before he'd realized Brooke was standing in the doorway listening to them. "Yes, well, he abandons the subtle approach when it's just the two of us," he remarked finally. He drank some more beer.

Brooke took a few seconds to chew a particularly elastic piece of mozzarella cheese. "Do you—" she began, then stopped herself. No. It was too personal a question.

"Do I what?"

"Nothing."

Meade put down his beer mug. His gaze was very sharp. "Ask me," he said quietly. "Whatever it is. Ask me. Please."

She shook her head, her hair swinging back and forth. "It's none of my business."

"How can you be sure?"

"How can I—because I am, that's how!" She dropped her eyes, studying her half-eaten slice of pizza.

Meade leaned forward and reached across the table. He cupped Brooke's chin in his hand and tilted her head up. "Look, Brooke. A week ago you said you didn't know me very well."

Brooke felt her cheeks heat up. "That's not exactly what I said."

"But it's what you meant. I understood. I *understand*. Believe me, I understand. Something happened to both of us when we were helping Jazz in the labor room. Oh, hell, why not be absolutely honest? Something happened to both of us when I opened my apartment door at twelve-thirty A.M. a week ago last Tuesday and we saw each other for the first time. I don't know what it was. I can't explain it. But I experienced it. I felt it. I *feel* it every time I look at you or touch you or think about you—"

"Meade—" The intensity of his words was turning her bones to jelly. She couldn't have gotten up at that moment if she'd wanted to.

"And it's the same way for you, too . . . isn't it." It was more of a demand for confirmation than an actual question.

Brooke didn't answer.

"Isn't it?" His hold on her chin tightened just a little, telling her that he would not stop asking until he got a reply.

Brooke ran the tip of her tongue over her lips. "Yes," she admitted after a moment. "But . . . it's still too fast, Meade. I'm sorry."

Meade studied her intently for several seconds as though trying to piece together a very complicated puzzle. Then the cup of his hand softened into a caress. He trailed his fingers lightly down the line of her throat.

"Never be sorry about telling the truth, Brooke," he said simply.

"So, what was your question?" Meade inquired casually about an hour later as he and Brooke walked home from the restaurant.

"My question?" Brooke echoed, puzzled.

"The one that was none of your business. Back at the pizza place."

"Oh. That question." There was a rock on the sidewalk. Brooke kicked it and sent it skittering on ahead of them.

"Yes, that question," he confirmed. Her reticence both intrigued and frustrated him. "What was it?"

As Brooke turned her head to look at him, an errant breeze sent a strand of hair blowing across her face. She grimaced and brushed it back behind her ear. "You're very persistent, aren't you?" she remarked.

"The preferred term is 'pigheaded,' and yes, I am." During the past week, Meade had seen the careful way Brooke shied from most personal questions. There was nothing coy about it. She did not, unlike a number of women he'd known, try to keep her secrets while delving into his.

And Brooke plainly had secrets. Nearly all of them, Meade was willing to wager his Ph.D. and his tenured teaching position, connected with her marriage.

Something more than desire gnawed at him every time he thought about the embrace they'd shared in the entrance foyer of his house a week ago. Brook had come out of his arms trembling with response . . . and resistance. The expression on her face had held a mixture of shock and sadness and yearning.

She'd been like a flame, shivering with sweet heat and temptation.

She'd also kissed with her lips closed quite tightly.

"Meade?"

The sound of Brooke's voice jolted him out of his reverie. He realized they'd both stopped walking. Taking a quick breath, Meade raked his thoughts together. He jammed his hands into the pockets of his jeans, trying to ignore the throbbing tightness in the lower part of his body.

He looked at Brooke. She was studying him with concerned eyes and a slightly furrowed brow. He wanted to soothe the anxiety and stroke away the pleated lines of strain.

"You'd better ask the question, Brooke," he said finally, keeping his tone light. "If you don't, I'm going to spend the rest of the night imagining what it was, and I'm pretty sure what I come up with will be a lot worse than the real thing."

Her eyes flicked back and forth for a second or two. Then she sighed. "All right," she responded. "I just—I wondered if you thought you would have gotten married and had children if your parents hadn't been . . . pushing you about it."

His brows went up. "Ouch."

"I told you it was none of my business!"

"No, no." Meade shook his head quickly. He wanted to tell her that, as far as he was concerned, anything she wanted to know about him was her business. But he held back. "It's just that it's been a while—" He gave a rueful chuckle. "My mother's usually the one who nails me with questions like that."

"You don't have to answer—"

"I know I don't have to," he assured her. "I want to. Yes, I think family pressure probably has put my back up a little where settling down is concerned. Less now than when I was younger, though. Of course, the pressure has always been well intentioned. But—" He shrugged.

"It's still been pressure," Brooke completed, almost to herself.

"Exactly," Meade agreed, wondering how much to read into her comment. He let a moment go by, then went on. "But, to be honest, if I'd truly been inclined toward getting married, I certainly wouldn't have balked at doing it because my parents happened to be shoving me down the aisle. No, my staying single has really been a result of my work and . . . well, I suppose you could say too-high expectations."

"Too high—?"

"Mmmm." He nodded slowly. This was not something he'd ever articulated, but it had been taking shape in his mind since he'd watched Brooke sleeping in his arms in the hospital alcove. "A lot of people I know say all they ever see are bad marriages. They check the divorce statistics, figure the odds are against them, and say 'Why bother?' But most of the marriages I know are damned good ones. I look at my parents. At what the professor and Gabrielle had. My two sisters and their husbands—"

"Ethan and Jazz," Brooke contributed quietly.

"Ethan and Jazz," Meade concurred. "Anyway. I'm not willing to settle for anything less than what I know is possible between a man and a woman . . . a husband and wife. It's that simple. Or that complicated, depending on how you want to look at it."

There was a break in the conversation then, and they began walking once more. Meade slanted a glance at Brooke. She seemed lost in contemplation.

"What's your family like?" he asked curiously. For all the time they'd spent talking together during the past week, he still knew only the most basic details about her background. He'd volunteered information about himself on a number of occasions, hoping to encourage her to open up; but the ploy had not proven very successful.

Brooke blinked. She hesitated for a moment, then he saw one corner of her mouth indent and curl upward. "Didn't you hear what I told your father?" she inquired mildly.

"Wha—oh."

"We got all the way back to my Mayflower ancestors." She was definitely teasing him.

"Yes, well—" Meade laughed. "All right. I admit I wasn't listening very closely. I was too busy trying to figure out how I could slap a hand over my father's mouth and hustle him out the door without being too obvious about what I was doing."

Brooke smiled. "Couldn't be done."

"So I realized. That's why I decided to remind him that it was getting late and he had to get home for dinner. My mother makes moussaka every Wednesday, and she turns very temperamental if she can't serve it at six-thirty on the dot. In any case—about your family?"

"Well . . . I think I told you I have one sister. My father's in insurance. He talks about retiring, but he never does anything about it. My mother plays golf and does a lot of volunteer work. They're . . . they're very nice people. Good people."

"Did they . . . push you about getting married?"

For a second or so, he didn't know whether Brooke was going to answer. Then she shook her head. "No," she said softly. "I did that myself."

"I don't understand."

Brooke sighed. "I never cared about having a career. Oh, I did well in school, and I enjoyed the jobs I had. But, ever since I was little, what I really wanted was to get married . . . to have children. Unfortunately . . ." Her tone turned flinty. "Unfortunately, you don't always get what you want."

"What about your husband? Your . . . ex-husband, I mean." Meade knew he was walking into mined territory, but he had to risk it.

Brooke looked down at the sidewalk. Her fair hair tumbled over her shoulders, covering her face. Meade clamped down on the desire to pull the pale curtain back and see the expression she was hiding. *Slowly,* he reminded himself. *You told her you'd go slowly.*

"Peter didn't get what he wanted, either," Brooke said in a voice that was as flat and as colorless as a pane of clear glass.

Meade was still weighing Brooke's quiet words when he got into bed that night. She could have meant many different things by them, of course; but, deep in his gut, he knew there was only one interpretation that explained the contradictions he'd sensed in her from the beginning.

Meade couldn't recall when he'd first heard the saying "There are no cold women, only clumsy men." It didn't matter. What was important was that he believed it held a great deal of truth.

The woman who had comforted Jazz Wilding with such passionate conviction was not cold. The woman who, although sometimes awkward and evasive, could make his blood go thick and hot with a single look or an unconscious touch was not cold, either.

Brooke Livingstone was warmth all the way through. But she didn't seem to know it.

And, as for her ex-husband . . .

Meade realized he'd clenched his fists. He forced himself to relax his fingers. He stared up at the ceiling.

He had a feeling Peter Livingstone had been much worse than clumsy. He had a feeling the bastard had been deliberately cruel.

Chapter 5

"I STILL CAN'T BELIEVE HOW much Jonathan's grown in just two weeks," Brooke said as she and Jazz walked slowly toward the front door of Jazz and Ethan's Back Bay brownstone. "He looked so tiny in the hospital nursery. But, now. . ." Her voice trailed off as she recalled what it had felt like to cradle her friend's sleeping, sweet-smelling baby in her arms.

"Well, considering that he's been nursing his little red head off, it's amazing he's not bigger," Jazz responded, smiling. "Ethan calls him Piglet."

"He does?" The image of one of Boston's most distinguished bankers behaving like a hopelessly doting daddy was very amusing.

"He does," Jazz confirmed. "When he's not 'gooing' or 'gagaing' or reading the baby stock quotations out of the *Wall Street Journal*. I, personally, think of Jonathan as the Gummy Bear."

"Jazz!" Brooke gave a choke of laughter.

"Of course, if he had teeth, he'd be Jaws," Jazz went on outrageously, her large gray eyes sparkling.

Brooke shook her head. "That's an awful way to talk about my godson-to-be," she declared in a tone of mock reproach.

Jazz wagged a finger. "You really fell for that little angel act of his, didn't you?" she teased.

"Well . . ." Brooke gestured. A jumbled wave of emotion swept over her, filling her heart in a way that was both painfully sad and poignantly sweet. "He's . . . he's so beautiful, Jazz," she said with deep feeling. *And you're so lucky*, she added silently. *So, so lucky*.

The gamine features of her friend's luminously happy face grew soft and serious. "He is, isn't he," Jazz agreed, then tilted her head slightly and studied Brooke silently for several long moments. "I'm so glad you and Meade agreed to be his godparents," she said finally.

"Oh, I'm so glad you asked me!"

Brooke had been deeply and truly touched when Jazz had broached the matter at the start of this Friday afternoon visit. She'd also felt a little strange—still did, in fact—about the very casual way Jazz had paired her name with Meade's when making the request.

"Who else would we—could we—ask?" Jazz wanted to know.

"Well . . . maybe someone from Ethan's family—?" Brooke suggested tentatively.

"No," Jazz replied firmly, her red-gold curls bouncing as she shook her head to underscore her answer. "Look, Casey and Laura stood by me and Ethan when we got married. You and Meade stood by us when we had Jonathan. We want the four of you to stand by our son when he gets christened. As for Ethan's family—well, it's no secret that the only ones I care about are his mother and father and Amanda, and they're all perfectly happy with our decision. So, if his sisters or any of the other Wildings feel they've been snubbed . . ." Jazz shrugged and pulled a face. "Ethan says most of them have been turning up their noses at the world so long they're permanently out of joint anyway."

Brooke smiled her understanding. She'd had only one brief encounter with Ethan's sisters, Emily and Enid, and that had been quite enough. "All right," she said. "It really does mean a lot to me."

"After what you did—" Jazz began feelingly, then broke off as there was a loud rumble of thunder. She glanced out one of the narrow casement windows that flanked the front door. "My God, it's *pouring*!" she exclaimed.

Brooke looked out, too. The sky had been overcast and spitting an occasional raindrop when she'd arrived at Jazz's about an hour and a half before. Now it was a dark, stormy gray and dumping down buckets. She said a silent word of thanks for the impulse that had prompted her to tuck a collapsible umbrella into her roomy shoulder bag before she'd left for work that morning.

"You can't go out in this," Jazz said flatly.

"Jazz, it's only rain. I won't melt."

"It looks awful. I think you should stay here until it lightens up. I know—stay for dinner! You can call Meade—"

"Meade?" Brooke questioned, stiffening. She said the name more sharply than she intended. "Why should I call Meade?"

Jazz gave her a slightly impatient look. "Because he'll wonder where you are if you don't. He's probably wondering right now."

"Jazz . . ." Brooke gave a little laugh. "I don't know what—Meade O'Malley doesn't keep track of my comings and goings. Just because we happen to be living in the same house . . . I mean, we're friends, of course. But he and I—we're not . . ." She stopped, then asked with an almost accusatory bluntness: "You—you think there's something going on between us, don't you?"

Brooke decided later that she shouldn't have been surprised by Jazz's reply. One thing she'd learned very quickly about her friend was that she believed in giving direct answers to direct questions.

"Uh-huh," Jazz replied with devastating simplicity.

"Well—" Brooke wondered what had happened to her ability to breathe normally. "Well—there's not!"

Jazz didn't say anything. There was another rumble of thunder.

Brooke's memory suddenly replayed the words she and Meade had exchanged a little over a week before . . . the words she had tried very hard to put out of her mind.

Something happened to both of us when we were helping Jazz in the labor room, he'd said. *Oh, hell, why not be absolutely honest? Something happened to both of us when I opened my apartment door at twelve-thirty* A.M. *a week ago last Tuesday and we saw each other for the first time. I felt it. I feel it every time I look at you or touch you or think about you—*

She'd spoken his name.

And it's the same way for you, too . . . isn't it. He'd been telling, not really asking.

She hadn't replied.

Isn't it?

Yes, she'd admitted. *But . . . it's still too fast, Meade.*

"Brooke?" Jazz asked, putting a hand on her arm.

Brooke looked at her friend. "I . . . that wasn't the truth," she admitted after a moment. "About there not being something going on between Meade and me."

Jazz's smile was wryly wise yet very gentle. "I know."

"But we're not—that is, it's not what you think it is," Brooke added hastily. There was another rumble of thunder. She grimaced. "What . . . what *do* you think it is?" she asked a trifle desperately.

Jazz seemed to take a long time considering her reply. When she finally spoke, it was in a tone of utter certainty. "Something special."

Brooke looked away for a second, staring at the rain

spattering against the window glass. "It hasn't even been three weeks . . ." she murmured.

"You sound like Meade."

Brooke's eyes snapped back to her friend's face. "He—you've been talking about me?" Meade had mentioned he'd visited Jazz when they'd seen each other—he coming in, she going out—that morning. But he hadn't said anything about—

"He asked me a few questions about you when he dropped by yesterday to see the baby."

"What . . . what did you tell him?" Brooke wanted to know, trying to keep her tone even and unedged. She hated the idea of people discussing her, dissecting her. She'd had enough of that during her marriage.

"Nothing he didn't know already. That you'd been married. That you got divorced. That I don't betray confidences." Jazz wrinkled her nose. "Not that you've confided all that much in me," she added after a moment.

The temptation to respond to Jazz's unspoken but obvious offer of a sympathetic ear was very strong. But Brooke's inhibitions against succumbing were even stronger.

She was desperately afraid that if she started talking, she wouldn't be able to stop. Everything she'd held inside her since the breakup of her marriage would come pouring out. Brooke didn't want that. Peter had hurt her terribly by making her failures public—by revealing what should have been private hurts to almost anyone who would listen. One thing Brooke had vowed when she came to Boston was that she was never going to allow herself to be so exposed, so vulnerable, again.

Beyond that, there was the fear that if she told Jazz about her inability to have a child, it would damage a relationship she'd come to value. She knew that Jazz's past unhappinesses had made her very sensitive to other people's pain. Brooke didn't want her friend to know that little

Jonathan Wilding was a source of hurt—as well as happiness—for her.

"Jazz—" she began, her throat tight. "I—"

"It's all right, Brooke," Jazz said, her cloud-gray eyes serene and steady. "I don't drag confidences out of people any more than I betray them. Sometimes talking helps. Sometimes it doesn't. I just want you to know you have a friend who's willing to listen."

Brooke smiled crookedly. "I know that. To—to tell the truth, it's one of the few things I *do* know for sure right now." There was yet another rumble of thunder.

Jazz returned her smile. "So, stay to dinner—friend?" she asked, repeating her earlier invitation.

Brooke shook her head. "No. No, I can't, Jazz," she refused. "But, thank you."

"You're positive?"

"Absolutely. Look—" She glanced out the window again. "I think the rain's starting to let up already. You know how these summer thunderstorms are. They never last very long."

"You don't have a raincoat or a hat," Jazz pointed out a bit anxiously. "If you go out without a raincoat or a hat, you'll get soaked and you'll probably catch a cold and—and—and, ohmigod! I sound just like somebody's mother, don't I?" She stared at Brooke, her expression half-pleased, half-perturbed.

Brooke laughed a little. "You *are* somebody's mother, Jazz," she reminded her friend. "But you didn't mention that I don't have any galoshes. I remember my mother used to nag me about wearing my rubbers every time it rained."

"Mmmm—" Jazz frowned for a second, possibly filing this bit of information away for future reference. "Well, what about an umbrella?" she demanded abruptly. "At least let me get you an umbrella—"

Brooke opened her shoulder bag. "It's all right, Jazz.

I've got one in here. My mother used to nag me about carrying an umbrella, too."

In a perverse way, Brooke was grateful for the bad weather. Navigating safely through the city's rain-snarled traffic required all her concentration. It enabled her to block, at least temporarily, the thoughts of Meade that kept trying to crowd into her mind.

She went across the Charles River at a snail's pace. Jagged streaks of lightning ripped through the slate-colored sky at irregular intervals. There were great claps of thunder, as though the heavens were auditioning for the percussion section in the Boston Pops' version of "The 1812 Overture."

"You know what these summer thunderstorms are like," she muttered, mocking her earlier comments as she squinted, trying to make out the road ahead. The windshield wipers squeaked back and forth in a mindless rhythm. "They never last very long . . ."

As if heeding her words, the rain seemed to lighten a little. She said a short prayer of thanks and turned onto Broadway. Not too much farther . . .

About three blocks from her home, her engine suddenly sputtered and cut out. It took Brooke a moment to realize what was going on, but she managed to steer the car over against the curb before it stopped moving.

"Oh, no, please don't do this to me!" she half pleaded, half protested. "I just had you in for a tune-up a month ago, remember?"

She turned the ignition key. The engine harrumphed several times, then fell silent. Brooke tried again. This time the engine gave a terminal-sounding rattle before stopping.

She shook her head. "All right, car," she said grimly. "I'm going to give you one more chance." She turned the key again, pumping the gas pedal and hoping that the third time would prove a charm.

The third time proved a total bust. The engine didn't respond with so much as a hiccup.

"Great!" Brooke exclaimed, hitting the steering wheel with her palm. Outside, a small tree branch smacked against her windshield. "Just great!"

She debated her options for a few moments, then decided to give the weather fifteen minutes to live up to New England's well-known reputation for climatological fickleness. The regional forces of nature repaid her patience by producing more rain than ever.

You can't stay in the car all night, she finally told herself, mentally measuring the distance she had to cover. It's only three blocks. You won't drown in three blocks. Oh, sure, you'll ruin the most comfortable pair of pumps you've ever owned and wreck an outfit you've only worn two times . . . but you won't drown.

She was thoroughly soaked within twenty seconds of leaving the car.

A powerful gust of wind inverted her umbrella and jerked it out of her hands as she completed the second block of her dash through the deluge.

Halfway across the front lawn of the house she lived in, Brooke slipped and went sprawling forward, landing hard on her hands and knees. Her shoulder bag fell open, its contents spilling out across the sodden ground.

It was at this point that Brooke began to think drowning might not be so bad after all.

"I f-feel like s-something the c-cat dr-dragged in," Brooke said miserably, trying to control the violent shivers running through her body.

"It'd have to be a pretty desperate cat," Meade told her wryly, steering her out of the entrance foyer and into his apartment.

"Th-thanks, M-Meade," she returned through chattering teeth.

"You're welcome."

Meade had heard Brooke pounding on the front door just about a minute before. Alarmed, he'd hurried to respond to her pleas to be let in. She'd stumbled out of the storm—and very nearly into his arms—gasping something about a dead car and lost keys. He'd experienced a few awful seconds before he'd assured himself that she was just soaked and shaken up, not seriously hurt.

"Wh-why—why is it so dark in here?" Brooke asked, trying to push a sodden hunk of hair off her face. She left a streak of mud on her cheek.

"The power's gone off," he explained. "Look. You go into the bathroom and take off those wet clothes, all right? I'll run up to your place and get you something to change into."

Brooke hugged herself. "You c-can't get in. My k-k-keys—when I f-fell—"

"I know. You said everything came out of your bag. But don't worry. I'm your landlord, remember? I've got an extra set of keys."

"Oh." Her green eyes, ringed by a smudging of mascara, dominated her fair-skinned face.

Meade put his hands on Brooke's slender shoulders and firmly turned her to the left. "The bathroom's that way," he said. "Go."

As he watched her make her dripping way across the room, he wondered whether she had any idea her dress was clinging to her body like a second skin and that he could make out every stitch of underwear she had on.

Brooke came out of Meade's bathroom about thirty minutes later feeling decidedly more human—to say nothing of a lot drier—than when she'd gone into it. She was swaddled from throat to ankle in a peach zip-front caftan.

Her face was bare of mud and makeup and her hair was finger-combed back off her brow.

Meade rose to his feet as she padded into the living room, setting aside the sheaf of research notes he'd been going through. "Recovered?" he inquired laconically, letting his eyes sweep over her. The fresh-scrubbed look became her.

Brooke nodded. "Yes, thank you," she said, shifting slightly under the stroke of his gaze. "I took a shower and washed my hair. I—I hope you don't mind." She glanced around. There were about a half dozen softly glowing kerosene lamps scattered about the room, creating appealing pools of illumination.

"No, of course not," Meade assured her with a smile. "Look, I've got some tea brewing in the kitchen. Why don't you sit down, and I'll get you a cup."

Brooke watched him leave the room with the catlike stride that was so much a part of him, then moved to settle herself on one of the sofas that flanked the stone fireplace. Her eyes strayed involuntarily to the cluttered table about a yard away. She focused, for just an instant, on the small, voluptuously carved figurine she recalled all too vividly.

She looked away, rubbing her palms against the nubby fabric of her robe, trying not to remember the ripely heavy feel of the statuette.

"Your tea, madam," Meade announced, returning from the kitchen. He was carrying a brightly glazed mug in one hand and a towel and a small jar in the other.

"Ah—thank you," Brooke replied, accepting the mug. "How did you heat—?"

"Camp stove."

"Of course." Brooke felt a bit foolish she hadn't thought it through for herself. "I should have remembered you're used to living without electricity."

"Well—" He grinned. "Let's just say that I've learned to manage under more primitive circumstances than these."

Brooke took a sip of the steaming brown-gold brew in the mug. It washed her taste buds with a delicious, slightly exotic flavor. "Mmmm. This is wonderful. What kind of tea is it?" She savored another sip, trying to puzzle out the possible ingredients.

"An herbal blend," Meade answered casually, seating himself at her feet with his legs folded tailor fashion. He waited a beat then added: "Plus a healthy slug of Napoleon brandy."

Brooke took a slightly larger swallow than she intended. "Herbs . . . and brandy," she repeated. The truth of his words was borne out by the sudden bloom of warmth in her stomach. "A recipe you picked up while learning to manage under primitive circumstances?" she suggested teasingly.

"Not exactly," Meade chuckled, spreading the towel he'd brought in from the kitchen over his knees. "I got it from a postgrad student I roomed with the summer I spent at Oxford. He was half-Chinese, half-French."

"Half—" Brooke blinked, abruptly registering the oddness of where Meade was sitting. "What are you doing on the floor?" she asked.

"I noticed when you came in that your left leg was scraped up. I've got something to put on it."

"Oh—you don't have to—" Brooke temporized, taken aback by the thought that he'd noticed what was a very minor injury. She hadn't even realized her fall in the front yard had cost her a strip of skin—plus a good pair of panty hose—until she'd gotten into the bathroom and started peeling off her wet, muddy clothes. "It's nothing, Meade. Really."

"Humor me," Meade said quietly, lifting the hem of her robe.

Brooke took a moment to gauge the determination in his expression, then decided she didn't have much choice.

Opening the jar of antiseptic ointment he'd brought out

with the towel, Meade studied the abrasions that ran down the length of Brooke's shin. It was obvious that her assessment of her injury was accurate. Still, nearly two decades of fieldwork made it impossible for him to ignore even the slightest physical hurt. He'd once seen a colleague come close to losing a hand because a cut on his palm had been dismissed as "nothing" and become dangerously infected after being left untreated.

"This may sting a little," he warned as he dipped the fingers of his right hand into the jar.

Brooke did experience a small tingle of discomfort as Meade started to stroke on the ointment. But it was swiftly lost in the sensations that arrowed through her as his left hand slipped around to cup the curve of her calf and hold her leg steady. She caught her breath.

"Sorry," Meade said, feeling her muscles tighten against his palm. He glanced up, frowning at the idea that he'd give Brooke any kind of pain. She was looking at him with wide eyes and slightly parted lips. "Brooke—?"

"It's all right," she told him quickly. "I—it's just—it *does* sting . . . a little."

He nodded slowly, then bent his dark head again and went back to applying the ointment with a featherlight touch. The expression he'd just seen on Brooke's face reminded him of the one he'd seen after he'd kissed her for the first time.

Meade had kissed Brooke several more times during the past week. And each time he'd kissed her, his conviction about what the physical side of her marriage must have been like had grown. Her instinctive responses to him shimmered with innate, untried sensuality. But there always came an instant, an instant Meade kept himself attuned to sense, when those responses were overridden by the force of experience.

Meade had never tried to hold Brooke when he'd felt

her start to withdraw. What he wanted from her had to be given freely or not at all.

"There," Meade said evenly, gently rubbing the last bit of clear antiseptic cream into her skin. He let go of her leg. "All done."

"Thank you," Brooke replied, pushing the hem of her robe back down.

"My pleasure," he told her, getting to his feet in an effortless upward surge. He studied her silently for several moments. "Would you like to stay for supper?" he asked suddenly, raking one hand back through his hair. He would never try to hold her against her will . . . but he'd damned sure try to keep her close to him.

Brooke tilted her chin so she could look up into his eyes. She could see the glow from out of the lamps reflected in their brilliant depths. A rumble of thunder sounded outside.

"Will I be able to pick up some pointers about managing under primitive circumstances if I do?" she inquired, lifting her brows just a little.

Meade's teeth showed white against his sun-darkened skin and he extended a hand to her. "Maybe one or two."

Chapter 6

"FRENCH BREAD, WINE, AND BRIE," Brooke mused aloud about two hours later, surveying the remains of the picnic spread out on the floor in front of her. She feigned a wistful sigh and glanced at Meade, who was sitting to her right. "I don't want to sound critical, Meade. But this really isn't my idea of primitive."

Meade looked at her. "Yes, I noticed how you had to force yourself to eat that third serving of pâté," he remarked. The gravity of his tone was at odds with the twitching of one corner of his mouth.

"We-e-e-ll . . ." Brooke dabbed daintily at her lips with a paper napkin. "I was hungry. Battling the elements gave me an appetite."

"'Battling the elements'?" he repeated, raising his brows. "What happened to 'surviving a hurricane'?"

"Oh, I realized it was the wrong season for hurricanes," Brooke said with a shrug, assuming the air of one for whom natural disasters are a minor inconvenience. She'd given Meade an absurdly and obviously exaggerated account of her three-block odyssey while they'd prepared their meal. He'd egged her on with ridiculous questions, encouraging her to produce a tale that had come out sounding like a cross between an old-time adventure serial and a PBS science special.

"Ah. Good point." Meade nodded his understanding, then cocked his head, listening to the storm outside. "You know, this *could* be a monsoon," he suggested teasingly.

"A monsoon?" Brooke echoed with delicate sarcasm. "Look, my weather expertise may pretty much be limited to knowing when to come in out of the rain, but even *I* know Massachusetts does not have monsoons."

Meade made a considering noise. "There's a first time for everything, Brooke," he replied. "There've been a lot of anomalies in the world's climate in recent years."

"And they're all due to fluorocarbons eating holes in the ozone layer, right?"

"Could be," he affirmed, stretching a little.

Watching him, Brooke could see the smooth ripple of his torso muscles beneath the fabric of his white knit shirt. She could also see the fan-shaped shadow of his dark chest hair. She reached for the nearly empty glass sitting on the floor next to her and drank the mouthful of wine left in it.

A few moments of silence slipped by. Then Meade commented: "You know, you're right. Pâté isn't very primitive. We probably should have gone ahead and roasted hot dogs in the fireplace."

"You told me the only hot dogs you have in the house are chopped up in cans of spaghetti and tomato sauce!" Brooke accused.

"Those *are* the only hotdogs I have," he conceded with a cheerful grin. "But just think how primitive fishing them out of the cold spaghetti would have been."

"Ugh." Brooke gave a small shudder.

"We could have pretended we were foraging through grubs."

"Meade!" She crumpled up her napkin and tossed it at

him. He batted it back to her like a badminton shuttlecock.

"Too primitive, hmm?" he challenged with a roguish wink.

"Exactly what I'd expect from a man who stocks his kitchen with Spaghetti-Os and Ring Ding Juniors," Brooke retorted.

"Now, now. I told you I keep that stuff around for my nephews."

So he had. He'd also told her that he kept three economy-size jars of extra-crunchy peanut butter on hand because a man came out of the rain forest with some strange, ah, *cravings*. Brooke hadn't been certain whether the tremor this word had touched off in her had been due to Meade's inflection or her unruly imagination. She still wasn't certain.

"Mmmm," Brooke said neutrally, shifting her position and fiddling with a lock of hair. "I wonder... I wonder what Jazz and Ethan had for dinner tonight."

"Oh, probably something extremely civilized," Meade returned. "Like snails." He studied Brooke for a few seconds, his senses suddenly alert to her change of mood. "Maybe you should have stayed to find out," he remarked quietly. She'd mentioned she'd been invited for dinner; she hadn't explained her reasons for refusing.

"No. I wanted to come home," Brooke said after a pause, still combing her fingers through her hair. She knew that Meade was watching her. She always knew. She'd always known when Peter was watching her, too. But this was different.

Meade O'Malley made her feel vulnerable. No. That wasn't quite right. He made her feel that it was safe to allow herself to *be* vulnerable. To touch... and be touched. Not just physically, although the past week especially had taught her some unexpected things about that; but emotionally, as well.

"Brooke?"

She looked at him. Somehow, during the last few moments, Meade had closed most of the distance between them. He'd been at arm's length before. Now he was near enough to touch . . . near enough to be touched.

Brooke eyes tracked slowly from the bold sweep of Meade's dark brows, down the arrogant line of his nose, to the well-defined shape of his sensual mouth. "Jazz thought I should call you," she said. "If I decided to stay to dinner."

Meade smiled a little, but the expression did not reach his blue eyes. They were serious and steady. "That might have been a bit of a problem, considering the phone went out along with the power," he told her. "But, I would have been relieved to know where you were. I started wondering around five-thirty. I was worrying by quarter after six."

"She—Jazz thought you would be."

"What did you think?"

Brooke moistened her lips with a dart of her tongue. "That you . . . probably don't keep track of my comings and goings."

"Fishing for compliments, Brooke?"

"N-no!" she denied. Something in his expression made her color. "No, of course not! Why—"

"Shhh, all right. I believe you." And the hell of it was, he did. Over the past two weeks, he'd become acutely aware of Brooke's peculiar combination of sensitivity and obliviousness. "Let me be the one to fish. Do you keep track of my comings and goings?"

Brooke's hand came up to her breast in an ancient and time-honored gesture of feminine protectiveness, almost as though she'd been caught half-naked. That Meade should ask her such a question shook her. That she should find herself wanting to answer it shook her even more.

"I know when you're here, Meade," she told him after a moment, feeling the flush in her cheek deepen. "And . . . I know when you're not."

Meade took a deep breath. He had not expected such an

admission. He'd barely let himself hope for one. Brooke's words affected him like an aphrodisiac. He let a few seconds pass, trying to steady himself. Then, he matched her honesty with his own.

"The only time I haven't known when you were in the house was that first night, when I was just back from Brazil," he said. "Since then . . ."

He lifted his right hand and traced the line of Brooke's cheek and chin. He stroked the pad of his thumb against her mouth, savoring the petal-soft texture of its rosy fullness. Her lips parted slightly and a tremor ran through her.

"Since then, even if I don't see you or hear you or smell your perfume, I know when you're home," he went on. "I can feel it, Brooke. I can feel *you*."

"M-Meade . . ." Brooke said shakily. Tiny sparks of excitement were flitting through her brain and bloodstream, mating and multiplying like fireflies. The power might be off, she thought, but there was no shortage of electricity in the room.

"I want to make love with you," he told her, his voice deepening. The force of his desire frayed the edges of his words. "But you know that, don't you. You've known it from the very beginning."

Brooke hesitated.

Never be sorry about telling the truth, he'd said.

"Yes," she whispered.

"I want to make love with you *now.* Tonight."

She swayed a little. Time seemed to slow . . . stretch . . . stop.

Meade cupped her face in his hands, his thumbs stroking her skin. "Tell me what you want, Brooke. Please. Tell me."

Brooke stared into his eyes. She'd been asked about her wants before, but she'd never really believed her answer mattered. This time, she did.

Never be sorry—

"Brooke?"

—about telling the truth.

"I want to make love with you, Meade. Now. Tonight."

It was the truth . . . as far as it went.

Meade led Brooke into his bedroom. It was a small room, furnished with almost Spartan simplicity. There were a few carefully culled books, several utterly plain stone pots, and an equal number of antique botanical prints. There was nothing extra. Nothing out of place. The clutter that characterized the rest of his rooms was absent.

Meade set down the lamp he had brought with him on an inlaid wooden chest just inside the door. The glow from it was soft and gently revealing. Brooke stood within the ring of illumination it created, watching him with wide, faintly shadowed eyes. He could see that she was quivering, like a reed in a strong wind.

Meade moved to her. He brought his hands up slowly and captured some of the hair that spilled over and around her shoulders like sunshine. He wove his fingers through the pale silk strands. He was close enough so he could see the pulse beating in the hollow of her throat. Close enough so he was sure she must be able to hear the sledgehammer thundering of his heart.

"Don't be afraid," Meade said softly. There was no more than an inch or two between them now. He could sense the warmth of her body beneath her robe and smell the heady scent of her clean-washed skin.

Brooke tilted her head back. The movement was languid, liquid . . . like slow-pouring honey. It was a movement of offering and affirmation.

"I'm not afraid," she answered, discovering the truth even as she spoke it. There were many things she was in this trembling moment of time, but afraid was not one of them.

Meade had not known how near the breaking point he

was until he heard her speak those three words. The rush of relief he experienced in response to them cost him more control than he could afford to lose. "Brooke—" he said, her name coming out half gasp, half groan. "Oh, God, Brooke—"

And then he kissed her.

The search of his mouth over hers was hot and hungry. Brook surrendered to it without hesitation, her whole body yielding to the lure of his masculinity. She opened her lips. An instant later, she knew the rough velvet sweep of his tongue. The taste of him flooded her, filled her.

Yes . . . oh, yes. Please . . . she thought.

Brooke's breathing pattern was short and shallow by the time they broke apart. She stared at Meade, mesmerized by the emotions she saw in the darkened depths of his sapphire eyes. It was not until his gaze started to move downward that she became aware that the front of her robe had been unzipped nearly to her navel. Cool air stirred tantalizingly over her heated skin. She felt her nipples begin to tighten.

"Oh, sweetheart . . ." Meade murmured, his voice a little hoarse. He gently slipped his hands inside her robe, defining the curve of her hip, the smooth indentation of her slim waist, and the burgeoning fullness of her partially bared breasts with his palms and fingers. He'd imagined doing this so many times . . .

What he'd imagined fell far short of reality.

It was not Brooke's way to be aggressive. She'd always been too uncertain to take the sexual initiative. But the bold stroke of Meade's hands on her body made the passivity of the past unthinkable—impossible.

The knit shirt Meade had on was tucked into snug-fitting jeans. Two tugs and it was free of the low-riding waistband. Then slowly, Brooke slid her hands beneath the garment.

She felt the shudder that ran through Meade in the first

heartbeat of contact and experienced a unique thrill of feminine excitement at the idea that her touch could stir him so deeply. She heard his breath catch, then release in a sound that could have been an invocation of her name. His skin was warm and smooth, the flesh beneath it firm. His well-toned muscles contracted as she moved her palms upward, discovering the crisp texture of his dark, whorling chest hair.

Brooke didn't know how long she indulged in her languid explorations. Nor did she know exactly when Meade's hands moved to begin peeling her robe back from her shoulders. The sudden shift of her hair against her naked skin alerted her to what was happening.

"I want to see you, Brooke," Meade told her huskily, the set of his features almost harsh. "Now." He slid the fabric that was covering her down a few more inches, then opened his fingers and let gravity do the rest. The robe fell straight to the floor, puddling around her slender ankles.

After a moment, Brooke took a step backward, moving out of the pool of material. For the first time, she felt a ripple of fear. Not fear of Meade. Fear of herself . . . of her inadequacies.

She did want to make love with him. Now. Tonight. She'd been telling the truth when she'd told him that. But it hadn't been the whole truth.

What she *truly* wanted was to please him. To please him in every way a woman could please a man. But that was something she was afraid she might not be able to do.

The sight of Brooke's fair-skinned nudity struck Meade like a molten fist. The tempting cluster of curls at the apex of her thighs was only a shade or two darker than the hair on her head. Except for the deep rose of her nipples, her body was a study in cream and honey.

He closed his eyes for a moment, struggling to draw breath, feeling as though all the oxygen had been sucked out of the room. Need clawed at him, demanding satisfaction. He'd wanted before, but never like this . . . never with such a primitive, primal hunger.

Slow down, goddammit. Slow down! he ordered himself.

"M-Meade?" Brooke questioned uncertainly, not knowing how to interpret the tension radiating from him. Had she done something? *Not* done something?

Meade opened his eyes. "You are so beautiful, Brooke," he told her. "So very beautiful. You make me feel . . ." He shook his head.

Brooke reached forward and brushed the tips of her fingers over his lips. "I hope . . . I hope it's what you make me feel," she whispered.

She had no memory of moving backward, yet she was suddenly aware that the edge of the bed was pressing against the backs of her knees. She sank down on it and waited . . .

It took only a second and a few sinuous movements for Meade to strip off his clothes and kick them away. Then he stood before her, completely naked and fully aroused. Seeing Brooke's expression as she looked at him, he spoke her name on a questioning note.

He felt her green gaze travel up his body the same way he'd felt her hands a few minutes earlier. When her eyes finally met his, she smiled. The curve of her lips was a little shy, but unshadowed by any hint of fear. After a few seconds, the shyness dissolved in the warmth of unmistakable invitation.

Meade joined her on the bed. Brooke flowed into his arms, filling them and all of his senses. He claimed her mouth in a slow, searing kiss. He courted her body with long, lingering caresses. He cupped her breasts, cherishing their fullness with his palms, teasing their sensitive crests with his thumbs.

Brooke gave a soft cry as his lips began tasting where his hands had touched. He nibbled and nuzzled one rose-tipped peak and then the other. She clutched at the back of his head, her fingers tangling in the thickness of his dark hair.

She let herself savor the delicious sensations Meade was evoking for many blissful moments. For each new pleasure, another two beckoned. It would be easy, oh so easy, to surrender and be selfish . . .

But Brooke couldn't do that. She wanted—needed—to give back some of what she was receiving.

Her desire was to offer pleasure. Instead, she seemed to provide something very like pain. When her soft fingers closed gently around the hard proof of his arousal, Meade's whole body went rigid. "Gah—Brooke!" he gasped. Her name sounded as though it had been torn out of him.

Shaking, Brooke jerked her hand away. A hot rush of shame hit her from one direction. A freezing blast of humiliation struck from the other.

"I'm—I'm s-sorry," she faltered.

Meade saw the sudden pallor of her cheeks and the sheen of hurt in her eyes. He realized in an instant that she'd misread his response. He cursed his lack of moderation. He'd reacted to her intimate touch because the erotic rightness of it had made him fear he was going to erupt like an untried boy and ruin everything.

"No, no, sweetheart," he said fiercely, catching her before she could withdraw any more than she already had. "Don't. It's all right. It's just that I want you so much, I don't have very much control right now. So, when you touched me the way you did—" He dipped his head and brushed his mouth over hers. Her lips were cool and closed. "It didn't just feel good, Brooke. It felt *too* good. I was afraid I was—things were going too fast. Much too fast."

"Too . . . fast?" Brooke echoed, trying to make sense of his words. Was it possible that she—*she*—?

"Yes. Yes, sweetheart," he affirmed huskily. "Remember? Like the first time we kissed?" He traced the outline of her lips with the tip of his tongue.

"I didn't—the way I touched you . . . you want that?" A touch of color had come back into her face.

"God, I'd love to have you touch me like that again," Meade answered feelingly. And I'd like to kill the bastard who made you believe that I—or any other man—wouldn't, he added silently. "But not just yet, Brooke. There's no need for us to hurry. We have all the time in the world. Let's go slowly . . . learn to know each other . . ."

He heard her give a shaky sigh and felt her body soften. Meade waited a moment, then gathered Brooke back into his arms.

Brooke wanted to please Meade. It was her deepest, most desperate desire. Her *only* desire.

She knew he was holding back. She could see the strain of self-control in his features, feel the stress of self-denial in his body. She could hear both in the shuddery rasp of his breathing. She knew he was holding back and she knew it was because of her.

There was no need.

"Please—" she entreated, expressing her desire with kisses and caresses. She could please him. She knew she could. He only had to let her.

Meade had wanted Brooke willing and that was what she was. Yet, even as he was responding to her erotic abandon, he was dimly conscious that something was not quite right. It was as though she was . . . was . . .

"Brooke—" Sweet heaven. Oh, sweet heaven! The womanly feel and fragrance of her made him wild. There was nothing about her that did not arouse and excite him. She was an irresistible temptation. All white heat and womanly allure.

Except—

A gnawing uneasiness made Meade move one hand

away from the roundness of her breast and down her rib cage. His palm slid across the flat plane of her stomach, absorbing the satiny texture of her skin as though he was addicted to it. The tip of one finger dipped briefly into the shallow indentation of her navel. Then he caressed lower still. Her thighs parted for him. Carefully, he tested the humid softness shielded by the triangle of her tight blond curls. His face went hard.

Whatever was driving Brooke, whatever was fueling the fever she seemed gripped by, it plainly wasn't an uncontrollable desire for him.

"Meade, please—" Brooke whispered, sensing his caution and his questions. She kissed the side of his throat, and nuzzled at the skin over the place where his pulse hammered.

"I don't want to hurt you—" Meade ground out, trying to ignore the provocative nibble of her teeth on the corded muscles of his neck. He was aware of his size and strength. He was also acutely aware that his usual ability to control himself was in shreds. If she wasn't truly ready for him . . .

"You won't," she assured him. "Please . . . now." And she moved her body against his in an invitation as old as Eve.

Meade's resistance broke. With a groan that acknowledged his flesh was all too willing as well as all too weak, he took what Brooke was offering. He filled her with a single sliding thrust. The joining of his hot hardness to her sleek softness nearly undid him, but he held on. The clasp of her flesh around his was very tight, much tighter than he'd thought possible. It provoked a pleasure so intense it was almost painful.

Meade forced himself to stay still, knowing that he was teetering on the brink. He wanted to find the key to bringing Brooke over the edge with him. Biting the inside of his cheek, he fought not to succumb to the clamor for release that was rising within him.

Brooke shifted slightly, her nails scoring lightly down the taut muscles of his powerful back. She lifted her hips as though to increase the intimacy of their fit. A strange flutter of sensation radiated from somewhere far inside her. It was like a summons to some unknown yet infinitely tempting new land.

"Not . . . yet . . ." Meade groaned, his fingers twisting convulsively in the sheets. "You—dammit—Brooke, I want you, too—" His voice was raw with frustration.

Until that instant, it had never occurred to Brooke that Meade might want to please her as deeply, as desperately, as she wanted to please him. It had never occurred to her that her pleasure could be his.

Meade shuddered. "I can't—I'm sorry—"

Brooke knew what she did then, as she felt Meade lose the battle he was waging on her behalf as well as his, was a lie.

She also knew it was an act of love.

Archimedes Xavier O'Malley had never been certain whether the question "Was it good for you?" had first been asked out of male arrogance or insecurity. Judging by the emotions that had prompted him to ask it in the past, he was willing to bet it had been a mixture of both.

Was it good for you?

Tell me I'm as terrific as I think I am.

Was it good for you?

In the name of heaven, reassure me that I wasn't the clumsy, selfish clod I'm afraid I may have been!

It had not been good for Brooke. She'd wanted him to think it had been, but he knew it had not. Even at the moment of ultimate release, when the ecstasy of his body had all but short-circuited his brain, he'd known it. And now, in the aftermath of that overwhelming experience, with his guts knotted with so many contradictory emotions he couldn't begin to untangle them . . .

Brooke sat up suddenly, holding the bedsheet to her breasts with tightly clenched fingers. Her hair tumbled down over her bare back like silver-gilt streamers. Meade could not see her face, but he could sense the tension vibrating through her. He could also hear the faintly ragged sound of her breathing.

Brooke brought her legs up and bowed her head, pressing her forehead against her knees. Her thoughts were hopelessly jumbled. She'd pleased Meade. She knew she had. And yet . . . and yet . . .

She had thought she'd find release. All she felt was restlessness. Instead of a much-yearned-for sense of fulfillment, she was experiencing a whole new kind of frustration. What was wrong with her? Why couldn't she—

"Brooke?"

She started at the sound of Meade's voice. She stiffened at the tentative brush of his fingertips against her upper arm. She was suddenly afraid she might start to cry.

She wanted. Oh, God, *she wanted* . . .

"Brooke," Meade repeated, his tone holding an odd combination of insistence and uncertainty.

She turned her head and looked at him. The expression in his eyes was so tender it took her a few seconds to recognize what she was seeing; it took her much longer to realize that the emotion was meant for her.

"Meade?" she questioned. Tenderness was not what she expected—what she had come to accept as inevitable—at a time like this.

Meade stroked her again, and felt a shiver dance just below the surface of her skin. Let me do this right, he prayed. For her sake . . . and for mine . . . let me do this right.

"You remember that conversation we had in the pizza place?" he asked her quietly.

Brooke was clearly bewildered by the inquiry. But, after several moments, she nodded.

"Good. Then you remember what I said about never being sorry—"

"—about telling the truth," she completed, her pupils dilating.

Meade knew he'd struck a nerve, but he didn't know how. He hesitated for a moment, then went on. "I meant it, Brooke. You should never be sorry about telling the truth about *anything*. Not about what you feel . . . or about what you don't feel."

"I—" Her throat closed up.

"You didn't—you don't—have to pretend. Not with me." His voice roughened on the last three words. He swallowed and repeated them in a gentler tone: "Please, not with me. Not now. Not ever."

Brooke averted her face then, the bitter taste of failure filling her mouth. For a moment, she thought of denying what he was saying. Of denying that her final response to him had been a sham. But she knew she couldn't. She also knew he wouldn't believe her if she did.

"All right," she said bleakly. "The truth. Not that you haven't figured it out for yourself. I'm not very . . . good . . . at making love. At—sex."

"They're not the same thing, Brooke."

Stung by what seemed to be the deliberate cruelty of this remark, she looked back at him. "Fine. I'm not very good at either," she told him tightly. And you, obviously, are an expert at both, she thought with a sudden pang of jealousy. You've probably known dozens of women—

"Brooke—" Meade saw the hurt return to her eyes with a kind of helpless rage. He hadn't meant—he'd only sought to make her understand that what they'd done together had not been—

"I wanted . . . I was trying to please you, Meade," she said with painful simplicity. "I know I d-didn't—"

"You know—" he choked. If he'd had any doubts about how badly she must have been used during her marriage,

what she'd just said wiped them out like a wet sponge erasing chalk marks from a blackboard. He allowed himself a split second to contemplate the savage satisfaction it would give him to break her ex-husband into tiny pieces. Then he purged that poisonous emotion and focused all his attention on Brooke.

"Sweetheart," he said, turning her so she was facing him directly. "Sweetheart, listen to me. If you'd pleased me much more, I'd still be in pieces."

She said something on a sharp intake of breath. A single syllable. It might have been his name.

"Yes!" he insisted, knowing she doubted him because she doubted herself. "You . . . pleased . . . me." He deliberately let the memory of the ecstasy he'd experienced in her arms color his words. Then he looked her square in the eye. "But I didn't please you, did I." It was not a question.

Her eyes widened with a queer kind of shock, her irises going very green. "That wasn't your fault!" she protested. She couldn't let him blame himself for her—

"Well, it wasn't yours, either," he replied instantly, unequivocably.

Brooke blinked. "It has to be *somebody's*—" she began.

"No, it doesn't," Meade interrupted gently. "Brooke, look. This is our first time with each other. First times aren't easy. Two people, coming together, trying to find one rhythm that works for both of them—no matter how well they know each other, how much they care . . ." He let a few moments go by, then continued speaking. "Maybe everything comes out right the first time in romantic fiction, but in real life . . ." He shook his head.

Brooke swallowed and looked down. "I haven't . . . there's only been one other first time for me," she confessed after several seconds.

Meade was not prepared for the violence of emotions he felt when he grasped exactly what she was saying. "Oh, Brooke . . ."

"I've never... never—" She faltered, then took a breath and looked at him. "I didn't want to pretend, Meade. I wanted—I *want*—it to be real. I—I wish... what you make me feel..." She gestured, trying to find a way to make him understand.

Meade slid his hands slowly up her arms and cupped her shoulders. Softly, steadily, he offered her the words she had given him earlier. "I hope it's what *you* make *me* feel," he said. He began to stroke his thumbs against her skin with small circular movements. "Because what you make me feel is that we can be good together, Brooke. Very, very good." The circles he was inscribing on her flesh widened. "Is that what you feel?"

Together.

Brooke thought of their first meeting... of the instant, almost inevitable eruption of attraction that had resulted. And she remembered the sense of bonding and connection she'd experienced when they'd helped Jazz give birth to her baby.

Together.

"Y-yes..." she said, her tone holding the same hint of surprise it had held when she'd told Meade she was not afraid.

"Good." The circling of his thumbs became a sensual sweeping.

"It's just that I've never..." She was struggling to unlearn the lessons of the past in order to accept the promise of the future. "Meade, I don't know if I can—"

"I do. You can." He touched her lips with lingering tenderness, then urged: "Trust me... *trust yourself.*"

With a sense of wonder, Brooke discovered that she could.

Slowly, very slowly, Meade eased Brooke back against the mattress. He combed his fingers through her hair, arranging it like flowing rays of pale sunlight. Dipping his head, he traced the curve of her brow with his lips. He nuzzled at her temples, feeling the throb of her pulse against his mouth. He nibbled at her ears, exploring their sensitive inner curvings with his tongue.

He kissed the delicate skin of her eyelids, the sudden flush on her cheeks, and the tip of her nose. Finally, he kissed her mouth. She yielded to him with a soft sigh, her warm breath marrying with his. After a heady moment, her tongue stole forward and flirted tantalizingly across his lips. Meade made a sound of surprise-laced satisfaction, then repaid her teasing tenfold.

His hands seemed to be everywhere. He explored her with long, languid sweeps. Excited her with brief, brushing touches. He made her body twist and turn, and his smile was very male as he gave her the caresses she was inviting. He plundered her responses like a pirate capturing a treasure, yet promised her more pleasure than she'd ever dreamed possible.

Brooke felt herself flowering like some exotic, fiery blossom. A sweet heat took hold of her, radiating through every fiber of her being. It was a delicious fever in which greed and giving held equal sway.

She tasted the hunger of his mouth . . . the hot salt tang of his skin. She tested the resilient power of his body, feeling his muscles ripple and bunch as she kissed and caressed him in every way her honey-fevered imagination could devise. She drank in the gasp he gave as she flicked her tongue lightly around the tightly furled button of his male nipple.

"Oh . . . Brooke . . ."

Meade molded the seductive shape of her hips, massaged the curving firmness of her bottom. Then he brought his hands up to claim her breasts, stroking the taut, rosebud peaks with his thumb. Brooke cried out, arching herself to fill his palms. She cried out a second time when he took one of his hands away, but the involuntary protest in the sound became something very different as she felt his mouth settle over her nipple and begin to suck. The slow, savoring tug of his lips was almost more than she could endure.

"Meade . . . please . . ."

The restlessness she had experienced earlier had metamorphosed into a raging wildfire. Brooke felt herself seeking . . . straining . . . reaching . . .

She was only dimly aware of Meade shifting himself, sliding down her body. It was not until she felt the hot stir of his breath against the trembling skin of her inner thighs that she realized his intention. She knew one instant of shock, and then that shock gave way to the most exquisite sensation she'd ever known as intention became intimate action.

Meade clasped her hips, holding her. He pleasured her with infinite care. Tenderly, he coaxed down the barriers . . . eased the restraints . . .

Brooke was in uncharted territory and she was burning. But she did not want to go up in flames alone. Reaching down, she tangled her fingers deep in Meade's hair and tugged. She wasn't certain she could speak. She wasn't even certain she could breath.

Meade's head came up, his eyes brilliant.

"Good . . . together . . ." were the only words Brooke could manage.

They were enough.

Meade moved up, over, and into her. His mouth came down, his lips brushing hers. Brooke wrapped her arms around him, holding him close, digging her nails into his shoulders as the first wave of ecstasy rolled over her.

It was her deepest desire to please him, and she did.

It was his deepest desire to please her, and he did.

But, in the last instant before she and Meade found a shared release, Brooke realized that the distinctions about who was pleasing whom had ceased to matter.

Chapter 7

SUNLIGHT AND THE SENSUAL DRIFT of Meade's fingers down her spine woke Brooke late the next morning.

"Mmmm . . ." she sighed, surfacing from slumber by increments. She sighed again, feeling the caressing nuzzle of Meade's mouth against the back of her neck. His warm breath eddied against her nape.

In a movement that was half lazy stretch, half languid shift, Brooke turned over to face her lover of one night.

"Good morning," Meade said quietly. He was propped up on one elbow, the drape of the bedsheet over the lower part of his lean body barely satisfying the demands of modesty. His hair was wildly disordered, some of it curving down over his brow like a comma. The shadowing of new beard growth on his jaw and chin gave him a rakishly sexy look.

His eyes, studying her from beneath heavy lids, were very blue and very tender. Brooke wanted to immerse herself in their compelling depths.

"Good morning," she replied, reaching up and brushing the errant lock of hair back from his forehead. She traced the strong, straight line of his nose with the tip of her index finger, then marked the hint of a smile that caused his lips to curl upward at the corners. It would have been impossible for her not to touch him.

Meade caught her hand and kissed her knuckles. "How do you feel?" he asked.

Sleep had tinted Brooke's cheeks a rosy pink. This color deepened in response to his question. At the same time, a very feminine glow came into her eyes. It made Meade think of sunlight streaming through the vibrant green leaves of a spring forest.

"I don't know," Brooke answered simply. She was conscious of a sweet sense of heaviness in her breasts and of a delicious ache of expectation low in her abdomen. She was more blissfully aware of her body than she had ever been in her life. "I . . . I've never felt the way I do right now." She gave a wondering laugh. "Does that make sense to you?"

"Oh, yes." Meade assured her with a knowing smile. He turned her hand over and kissed the fragile skin of her inner wrist. He felt the jump of her pulse against his mouth. "You see, sweetheart, I've never felt the way I do right now, either."

She caught her breath. "Really?"

"Really," he affirmed.

"Meade, I never knew—" she began huskily, then stopped as words failed her. How could she explain what she'd learned about herself—about him?

Releasing her hand, Meade stroked the smooth curve of her cheek. Brooke turned her face into his palm as though she wanted to prolong the caress. Meade sensed it was a completely instinctive action on her part, and he took a fiercely male kind of satisfaction in her responsiveness.

"I understand," he told her.

Brooke veiled her eyes with her lashes for a second or two, seized by an unfamiliar urge to flirt. "If *you've* never felt this way and *I've* never felt this way..." she mused reflectively. "Does that mean we're having our *second* first time together?" She slanted him an up-from-under look that defined the word *provocative* better than any dictionary.

The teasing question and the tantalizing glance combined to cause Meade's heart to slam against his chest so hard he was amazed it didn't crack a rib.

"Something like that," he agreed, emotion roughening the edges of his answer. His hand slid from her face, down the slim column of her throat, and slipped beneath the cotton sheet that shielded her body from view. He watched Brooke's eyelids flutter closed as he began to fondle the tip of one breast. Her nipple hardened in a matter of moments, peaking in answer to the coaxing finesse of his fingers. She made a soft sound of pleasure as he transferred his attentions to her other breast. He saw her nostrils flair on a sudden intake of breath.

"Oh, Meade..." she murmured.

Meade could feel the heat of desire rise in him. He could feel the renewal of a hunger that seemed to get stronger each time it was satisfied.

After a few moments, he flung back the sheet.

Meade realized he didn't have to ask. Brooke was already offering.

"There's something we need to talk about, Brooke."

Brooke lifted her head from his chest, her hair swinging forward in a heavy curtain of silk. She'd been listening to the rhythm of Meade's heart, hearing it go from the thunderous aftermath of sexual climax to the slow, steady beat of normalcy.

"Food?" she suggested hopefully, her eyes straying briefly to the clock next to Meade's bed. The power had come back on some time before and it was running once again. Unfortunately, it needed to be reset. While a certain hollowness in her stomach said lunchtime, the clock read six-thirty A.M.

Meade's mobile mouth twisted slightly as he acknowledged the fact that man could not live on lovemaking alone. "We'll get around to that," he promised.

"Ah—how about retrieving my car?" Shifting, Brooke shoveled several handfuls of hair back over her shoulders.

"We'll get around to that, too." Meade stroked his palms up the graceful line of her naked back. "This is . . . important."

Brooke opened her mouth to tell him that, from her point of view at least, both of the subjects she'd just put forward *were* important. Then she registered the seriousness of his expression. The impulse to tease died. A sudden tremor of anxiety ran through her.

"What . . . what is it, Meade?" she asked quietly.

Meade felt her quiver and heard the sudden tension in her voice. He cursed the fact that the only way he knew how to address the matter that needed addressing was head on.

"I didn't take any precautions with you, Brooke," he told her bluntly.

Something knotted inside Brooke's throat as she realized what he was saying. Her slender fingers, splayed flat against his chest, tightened. She moistened her lips.

"You mean . . . birth control," she said after a few moments.

"Protection," Meade expanded. "I didn't use anything and I didn't stop to ask you—" He shook his head, offering no excuses. He'd been careless with a woman who mattered very much to him, and it troubled him deeply.

Dropping her eyes, Brooke swallowed hard. The knot in her throat descended to her stomach. It sat there, cold and tight.

Meade had unwittingly given her an opening to reveal the full truth about herself. All she had to do was tell him that any worry about pregnancy was unnecessary because she was incapable of conceiving. It would be very simple. Just a few words . . .

Just a few words, but she couldn't say them. *She couldn't!* It wasn't that she feared he'd scorn her the way Peter had. She knew, with every fiber of her being, that Meade was incapable of such cruelty. What she was afraid of was having him feel sorry for her . . . of having him pity her. She knew she must have betrayed to him a hundred times over how she felt about children. If she told him she couldn't—

"Brooke?" Meade tilted her chin up. "Sweetheart, I realize this is awkward—"

"No . . . no." She shook her head, her decision made. She couldn't bear to expose her inadequacy. Not to him. Not now.

"No, what?" Meade probed gently, trying to understand the look on her face.

"No, it's not awkward," she said slowly. "Not . . . I mean, it shouldn't be. You're right, Meade. This *is* important. People—we have to care about consequences."

"It's *you* I care about, Brooke," he replied. The words were tender, but threaded with concern.

"I know," she answered, tracing a design in the thicket of his coarse silk chest hair. He'd demonstrated his care in in countless ways during the heady, heated hours of the night and early morning. "But, you don't have to be concerned about not protecting me. I—I'm . . . safe."

For a moment, he seemed to stop breathing. "Safe?"

"I'm on the Pill." This, at least, had the virtue of being the truth. Her doctor had prescribed the birth control pill as a means of regulating her extremely erratic cycle.

"Ah," was all Meade said.

Brooke thought he sounded relieved and told herself she'd done the right thing. After a few moments, she lowered her head, bringing her cheek back to rest on his sleekly muscled chest. She felt the slow glide of his hands and sighed. She shifted, fitting her soft woman's body against his much harder male one. She closed her eyes.

She'd done the right thing.

"Does your tattoo have a special meaning?" Brooke inquired curiously several hours later. They were in his kitchen fixing omelettes. Retrieving her car was next on their agenda.

"It's the markings of the *surucucu da jucca depico*," Meade answered, chopping a tomato with quick, deft strokes.

"The *what*?" Brooke paused in the act of pushing up the sleeves of her peach-colored robe and gave him a raised-brow look of inquiry. He was wearing a pair of jeans and nothing else. The wash-faded denim clung to his taut buttocks and long, lean flanks like a coat of blue paint. For a moment, Brooke completely forgot about his tattoo.

Meade repeated the name. "It's a South American snake," he explained, finishing with the tomato. He reached for a green bell pepper and began seeding and slicing it with surgical precision. He wielded the knife as though it were an extension of his hand.

"A snake." Tearing her eyes away from his body, Brooke completed the adjustment of her sleeves and began cracking eggs in a stainless steel bowl. "Is it—is it dangerous?"

"Deadly. Its venom attacks the central nervous system."

"Charming," Brooke commented. She debated whether she should use six or eight eggs. A growl from her stomach made her decision easy. "What a nice thing to have on your back."

"Actually, some Indian tribes consider it a very powerful protective symbol."

"Oh?" She recalled what he'd once told her about having a tendency to "go native" when working in the field. "Is that why you had it done?"

Meade gave her a sidelong glance. "I study tribal magic, Brooke. I don't practice it," he said wryly.

"Oh, no—" She shook her head quickly and made a gesture of denial with one eggy-fingered hand. "I didn't mean that, Meade! I just wondered if, well, if you considered it a—a—a good luck charm. Like a rabbit's foot or something."

He grinned. "The *surucucu da jucca depico* beats a rabbit's foot all to hell, believe me. The truth is, I can't remember why I had it done. Two friends and I got ingloriously drunk roughly twelve years ago in Rio during Carnaval. One of them woke up with a Superman logo tattooed on his chest; the other had a heart with the name of a woman he'd never heard of needled into his, ah, hindquarters. Frankly, I think I was lucky to get the snake."

Frankly, Brooke told him, she had to agree.

The next two weeks were rapturously happy ones for Brooke. Friendship intertwined with physical passion to create a relationship so fulfilling it almost took her breath away. There was laughter and there was loving . . . a meeting of minds as well as a merging of bodies.

She thought, a number of times, of telling Meade about her inability to have a child. But she couldn't find the right moment . . . the right words. Twice, in the tender aftermath of lovemaking, she came very close to whispering her secret to him. Yet, on both occasions, something held her back.

Brooke argued with herself that it didn't matter. Her infertility had no bearing on what she felt for Meade—on what she hoped he felt for her. She was giving him what he wanted . . . needed. She knew she was! Why tell him she couldn't give him something he'd never asked for?

Still, it gnawed at her. Nagged at her. Finally, she tried

to broach the matter obliquely, by bringing up her failed marriage.

Meade, to her astonishment, closed the door on the discussion.

"Please, Brooke," he said, shaking his head. There was a look in his eyes she'd never seen before. She saw his fists clench. "Don't."

"But, Meade, I—I want you to know—"

"I do, sweetheart. Believe me. I know you loved Peter Livingstone enough to marry him. I know he hurt you enough to make you doubt yourself as a woman. I also know I'll probably knock his teeth down his throat if I ever meet him." His mouth twisted. "It's primitive, not pretty, but it's the way I feel. It's also the reason I don't want to hear about your marriage. I'm sorry."

Brooke didn't know what to say to that, so she said nothing.

"Wilding Institute, would you hold the line for a moment, please?" Brooke requested crisply, one neatly manicured finger poised above the row of buttons on her phone.

"I'd rather hold you," came the provocative response.

"Meade?" she asked throatily.

"There's someone else in your life who makes comments like that?"

She laughed, feeling the burden of an incredibly heavy Friday morning workload lift. "Not that I recall, no. Look, can you hang on? I've got a call from a Japanese mountaineer who says he doesn't want to fly over for WIWE's next conference. He's insisting we book passage for him on a boat. Preferably the QE Two."

"Don't tell me. Dobie Tanaka, right?"

"Ah—" Brooke consulted the pad in front of her. "Tadeo Onoshi Tanaka, actually."

"That's the man."

"Do you know him?"

"Only by reputation. He won't fly because he's afraid of heights."

"He's afraid of—Meade, for heaven's sake, the man climbs mountains!"

A rich chuckle came through the line. "Supposedly he started doing that to overcome his fear. A matter of face."

"Face. Terrific. That explains everything. Look, I've got to put you on hold."

"I'll be here."

Armed with the insight Meade had provided, Brooke was able to deal with her overseas caller with dispatch. She also did so without once mentioning the word *acrophobia*. By the time she hung up, Tanaka was making fulsome comments about her gracious understanding and efficiency.

She hit the blinking call-waiting button on her phone. "Meade?" she asked eagerly.

"Back so soon?"

"What can I do for you?"

"Over the phone? Hmmm. Well, you *could* repeat what you said to me last nigh—"

"Meade!" she protested. Their love talk had been shamelessly uninhibited the previous evening. Meade had been erotically explicit in his verbal admiration of her body and she, surprising herself, had responded in kind.

"Well, then, how about making those sexy little moans—"

"I do not *moan*—" Brooke began to object indignantly. She broke off as she realized that Daniel Quincy was standing in the doorway to her office. She felt a wave of hot color surge from her throat to her hairline. "Hold on," she said to Meade, then covered the telephone mouthpiece with her hand. "Yes, Mr. Quincy?" she inquired. She strove for her usual polite and professional tone. She had to settle for slightly breathy and barely steady.

"I just wanted to tell you I'm leaving for lunch,

Brooke," WIWE's supremely dignified executive director informed her.

"Oh. Fine. Ah, thank you. Have—have a pleasant meal."

"Thank you, I intend to." Quincy's brows, which resembled a pair of silver caterpillars, lifted a bit. "Is that Meade O'Malley you're talking to?"

"Um—yes," Brooke confirmed.

"Mmmm. Please give him my regards. And tell him I'm interested in seeing the rest of his notes from the Xingu Basin when they're written up." He nodded at her in characteristically courtly fashion, then turned and began to walk away with a stately stride.

"I, ah, will, Mr. Quincy," Brooke said to his retreating back. She waited until he was out of earshot before uncovering the phone. She groaned.

"No-o-o-o," Meade drawled outrageously. "That's not quite the sound I had in mind, Brooke. It was more along the lines of—"

"W-will you p-please *stop* it!" Brooke sputtered. "Do you realize Mr. Quincy just heard me talking about moaning? And he knew it was you on the other end of the line, too, Meade. God only knows what he's thinking."

"More like only the Devil. Daniel is supposed to have been a real hellion with the ladies in his salad days."

"So I've heard." Brooke looked up into the beady glass eyes of the vulture that was suspended over her desk by a pair of wires. The stuffed bird was just one of countless eccentric or exotic touches that enlivened her work space and the rest of the WIWE offices. All of the items—ranging from an incredibly ugly elephant's foot umbrella stand to an exquisite ebony and ivory abacus, from an Egyptian mummy case to an American Indian war bonnet—were tokens of appreciation from the men and women who had enjoyed the institute's moral or monetary support over the past century.

In the beginning, Brooke had been slightly unnerved by the feeling of having a vulture—albeit a stuffed one—circling over her head. Gradually, however, she'd gotten used to it. Her only objection to the bird at this point was that it had started molting several weeks before. She was tired of plucking black feathers off her desk every morning.

"Brooke?"

She started. "Ah—yes. Sorry. What do you wa—I mean, why did you call?"

"No more straight lines, hmm?" he teased, making it plain he knew why she'd rephrased her question.

Brooke had to smile. "Meade, please. I've got a ton of work left. If you still want me to meet you for dinner—"

"Actually, that's why I'm calling. I seem to have acquired custody of my nephew, Kevin, until tomorrow."

"Oh?"

"It's a complicated story. His sister's having her first boy-girl party tonight and the last thing she wants is her kid brother underfoot. Kevin was supposed to spend the night with a friend, but that fell through. Normally, my parents or my sister Kathleen would take him, but they've all got plans."

"So, it's Uncle Meade to the rescue?"

"Something like that. Look, I know I promised you an elegant dinner in some intimate little restaurant. But, would you be willing to settle for an evening out with the guys?"

Brooke hesitated. She didn't want to intrude. "You don't think Kevin would mind?"

"Well, the fact that you're a girl—"

"Why, Meade, when did you realize that?" she inquired in a dulcet voice.

"Mmmm, I had my suspicions from the start. But seeing you in the shower the other morning was the real tipoff."

A delicious shiver of remembered pleasure rippled through Brooke's body. She and Meade had made love beneath the gushing water with a passionate yet playful abandon. At one point, she'd found herself caught between the cool, slick surface of one of the tiled shower walls and Meade's hot, hard body. The contrast in textures and temperatures had been arousing in the extreme. She'd never imagined herself doing—

"That's the sound."

Brooke came out of her sensual flashback with a start. "Ah—wh-what?" she asked. She really was going to have to do something about her recently discovered tendency toward erotic daydreams. Just the other day, she'd drifted off while proofing the galleys of a new monograph. She'd snapped to only to find she'd made some decidedly X-rated doodles in the margins.

"The sound you just made." Meade's voice was laced with amusement. "That's the kind of moan I was talking about a few minutes ago."

"Oh." She shifted in her seat. "Um . . . well. Yes. Anyway. You were saying something about my being a, ah, girl—?"

Meade chuckled. "Okay. I won't mention the moaning again. As I was saying, the fact that you're a female isn't exactly a point in your favor where Kevin is concerned. However, he's willing to overlook it—he's only eight, he can do that—since I vouched for you as a friend. There's two things I should warn you about, though. First of all, whatever's on Kevin's mind tends to come out of his mouth. And second, his idea of a great time is going to some godawful action movie and then chowing down on burgers at the local scarf-and-barf. So, would you like to join us tonight?"

Brooke laughed. "It sounds utterly irresistible."

Utterly irresistible was a pretty accurate description of eight-year-old Kevin Cunningham, too.

"So, what did you think of the movie, Kevin?" Brooke

asked him. They were sitting in a booth at a fast-food restaurant, waiting for Meade to return with their meal.

Kevin wrinkled his freckled nose. "It was good 'cept for the kissing stuff," he said. "It's okay to have one mushy scene, 'cuz when it's on you can go to the bathroom or maybe get some popcorn, you know? But not *three*. Three's way too many. Course, the girl got blown up by the bad guy, so it was okay in the end." He gave Brooke an engaging gap-toothed grin.

"I see." Brooke nodded, suppressing a laugh.

"The hero was pretty neat, too," Kevin went on consideringly. "But not as neat as Uncle Meade. Uncle Meade's *awesome*. You should see this terrific drum he brought me back from Brazil. I told him I wanted a shrunken head, but the drum is much better. Did you know he let me bring him to school for show-and-tell once? Boy, was *that* great. First he did these magic tricks. Like making coins disappear and fire dance on his fingers and stuff. Then he gave this talk about what it's like being in the jungle and studying plants. He told how some medicines we think are scientific really come from witch doctors! Even Sister Mary Agnes was impressed. She let him stay for the *whole morning*. We got to skip spelling."

"Sounds pretty terrific," Brooke commented. It had become very obvious very quickly that young Kevin absolutely worshiped his uncle. Equally striking to Brooke was the easy, open affection Meade lavished on his nephew. Yet it was clear to her that Meade was much more than an indulgent uncle. She'd seen him quell Kevin's rambunctiousness with a single word and a quick shake of his head. The youngster had accepted the discipline without protest or resentment.

"Uncle Meade says you know about some of the stuff he does 'cuz of your job," Kevin said in an approving tone. "You work at that whatchacallit—that Wildman Institution place, huh."

"The Wilding Institute for World Exploration," Brooke amended with a smile. "People call it WIWE for short."

"WIWE," the boy repeated, snickering in apparent amusement at the acronym. Then he cocked his cowlicked brown head and regarded Brooke with curious brown eyes. "You're the first lady to live in Uncle Meade's house, you know," he remarked.

"Oh . . . really?" Brooke wasn't quite sure how she should reply to this artless observation.

"Yeah," he affirmed with a bobbing nod. "I guess maybe that's why everybody's wondering about you."

"Everybody—?" Brooke stiffened.

"Uh-huh." Kevin nodded again. "That's one reason I told Uncle Meade it would be okay if he brought you with us to the movie and stuff. So I could meet you before almost anybody else." His eyes lit up with gleeful anticipation. "Boy, it's going to be ha-ha on a lot of people when they find out, too. Like my dumb sister Sarah. You know, I told you about the big stuck-up deal she made about not wanting me to be around for her stupid party tonight? As if I'd go, even if she invited me. Hah! Anyway, *she's* going to be *wicked* mad when I tell her about you, Miss Livingstone. Mom, too, I bet. And Aunt Kathleen. And maybe even Grandma O'Malley!"

Brooke felt as though she'd missed a connection. *Several* connections, in fact.

"Ah, why should they be mad—" she started.

"'Cuz, like I said, they're all really curious about you," the boy informed her, leaning forward a bit. "It started after Grandpa O'Malley met you. He liked you, you know. Did you like him?"

"Well, yes, I did, Kevin," Brooke admitted. "But—"

"That's good." He nodded, visibly pleased. "You'll prob'ly like Grandma O'Malley lots, too. She's more quiet than Grandpa, but she's really nice. *Anyway,* like I was saying, everybody wants to find out stuff about you. Like when Mom brought me over today, she was kind of nosy, you know? She gets that way sometimes and usually Uncle Meade just laughs about it. Only today I *think* he was sort of—uh—oh, hi, Uncle Meade! Did you get me double fries?"

"Double fries and triple ketchup," Meade answered, plunking down a food-laden plastic tray in the center of the table. He slid into the booth next to Brooke, moving close enough so their thighs brushed. "What did you think I was 'sort of' today, Kev?"

"Huh?" Kevin's forehead furrowed for a second, then smoothed out as he realized what his uncle wanted to know. "Oh! I thought you were sort of chewed out 'cuz Mom was asking you questions about Miss Livingstone," he answered offhandedly.

Meade glanced sideways at Brooke. "I see," he said. She thought there was a hint of apology in his tone. There was definitely a look of concern in his eyes.

"I told Miss Livingstone everybody's all curious 'cuz she's living in your house," Kevin continued blithely, rapidly sorting out the food on the tray. He seemed to annex three items for himself for every one he apportioned to Meade and Brooke. "Like the other Sunday when everybody came to Grandma and Grandpa O'Malley's house for dinner and you went away early, 'member? Well, I didn't tell you this before, Uncle Meade—but I was kind of hanging around outside the kitchen and I heard Mom and Aunt Kathleen and Grandma O'Malley talking about you and Miss Livingstone. Grandma O'Malley was saying something about wanting to ask Miss Livingstone for dinner and Grandpa O'Malley telling her she shouldn't 'cuz it would be a busybody thing to do. Then there was this stuff I didn't really understand. Finally, Aunt Kathleen said this weird thing bout your being a rolling stone who doesn't gather moss. So, I came in and said huh-unh, you did too.

Gather moss, I mean. In the jungle, right? That's your job. Course, not *just* moss, but—"

"Kevin—" Meade began. Brooke saw a flush darken the skin that covered the ridge of his cheekbones. She wasn't certain whether the heightened color was due to irritation, embarrassment, or a combination of both.

"Anyway—" the youngster plowed ahead, shoving a cup and straw at Brooke. "Here's your soda, Miss Livingstone. Do you want to share my fries? I got lots of 'em."

"Ah, thank you, Kevin," Brooke responded faintly, aware that her own face was a little pinker than normal, too.

"Kevin—" Meade tried again.

"You can eat some of my fries, too," Kevin informed his uncle generously. "Anyway, Mom got mad 'cuz I guess I was interrupting and she said she'd paddle me if I didn't go outside right that very instant. I could tell she wasn't kidding. So, I went out to play." He shrugged and began unwrapping his hamburger. "I didn't hear any more, Uncle Meade."

"Uncle" Meade muttered something under his breath. Brooke was pretty certain it involved thanking God for small favors.

"Alone at last," Meade said dramatically about thirty-six hours later, sitting down on one of his living room sofas and pulling Brooke onto his lap.

"Mmmm . . ." Brooke tilted her head, feeling the tantalizing nuzzle of his lips through her hair. He nipped gently at the side of her neck, sending a cascade of shivers coursing beneath the surface of her skin. "I—mmmm. I, ah, liked your sister," she remarked, feeling she should make some comment about the woman who'd just left.

Mary Margaret O'Malley Cunningham had proven to be a small, superenergized redhead several years older than Meade. While she looked nothing like her brother—indeed, Brooke had found their physical dissimilarities quite striking—the bond of affection between them had been a palpable thing. Equally obvious, and rather amusing, had been Mary Margaret's almost mother-hen manner toward her self-sufficient sibling.

"That's good," Meade returned wryly. "I've got another one just like her."

"You don't think she minded Kevin asking me to dinner next Saturday, do you?"

"Are you joking?" Meade grinned. "I'd be tempted to think she put him up to it except for the fact that Kevin probably would have prefaced the invitation by saying 'My mom wants me to ask you over to our house so everybody in the family can get a look at you' if she had."

"Hmmm..." Brooke responded neutrally. Kevin's mother had been openly curious about her during their brief encounter. Yet, as in the case of Francis O'Malley, her unabashed inquisitiveness had been tempered by a great deal of charm. "Have you . . . have you talked to your family about me?" she queried.

Meade clasped his hands together around her waist, loosely interlacing his fingers. "I've told them that you're someone very special," he said honestly. "I've also told them that you're a lady who doesn't like to be rushed."

"Oh." She veiled her eyes with her lashes, contemplating his words.

"You, ah, do realize what you're letting yourself in for, don't you?" he asked after a few moments.

Brooke turned so she could look at him. "By accepting your sister's invitation, you mean?"

He nodded.

"Would you rather I turned her down?"

The expression in Meade's blue eyes was warm and very direct. "No," he answered frankly. "I want you to meet the rest of my family, Brooke. They're very important to me. But, taken as a mob, they can be a little overwhelming. I don't want you to be . . . uncomfortable."

Brooke smiled a little. "You'll be there with me, won't you?"

"Oh, yes." It was a promise.

"Well, then, I won't be uncomfortable," she said simply.

It seemed to Meade there was only one possible response to that sort of answer. He gathered Brooke close and kissed her.

Closing her eyes as Meade's lips moved over hers, Brooke blissfully savored the taste and textures of his mouth. She brought one hand up to cup the back of his neck in the curve of her palm. She was aware of him capturing her hair in his fingers, and winding it around until he could control the movements of her head.

The kiss deepened and Brooke felt the delving stroke of his tongue. She responded with a flirtatious parry of her own. Meade gave a predatory-sounding growl and sucked her tongue into his mouth. The strong, suctioning tug triggered a fluttering contraction inside her midsection.

Meade exhaled on a short, harsh breath when they finally broke apart. "God," he exclaimed, very conscious of their contact. "I've been wanting to do that since yesterday."

Brooke altered her position slightly. She laughed a bit breathlessly. "It's probably just as well you waited."

"Oh?" He cocked one brow.

"Mmm-hmm. I think Kevin's extremely high opinion of you would have suffered if he'd caught you doing 'mushy stuff.'"

"You're probably right," Meade agreed. His gaze settled on her kiss-rouged lips. Brooke saw the blue of his eyes darken to midnight. When he spoke again, his voice was husky. "It's probably just as well I waited to do this, too—"

Bending his head, Meade began brushing his mouth

back and forth over Brooke's, creating an exquisite friction. Slowly, he increased the intimacy of the kiss, using his tongue to tease and tempt. Brooke's lips parted like a flower opening to the sun.

Brooke shifted her weight, shimmying her hips just a bit as she did so. She brought her hands up, locking them behind Meade's neck and tunneling her fingers deep into his thick, dark hair. Her soft breasts pressed against the wall of his firmly muscled chest. She breathed in the musk-male fragrance of his skin.

Meade planted a line of brief, burning kisses from Brooke's mouth to her ear. He tugged at the pretty floral cotton top she was wearing, pulling it free of the softly gathered matching skirt that was hiked up well above her knees. Guided only by touch, he found the buttons that marched up the front of her blouse. He began undoing them, one by one. His fingers were less than steady.

"Do you have any idea what it did to me last night?" he questioned, his lips moving against her ear. Brooke quivered at the caressing fan of his breath. "Knowing you were just upstairs . . . knowing we couldn't . . ." He gently raked the serrated edge of his front teeth over the sensitive flesh of her lobe as he finished opening her blouse.

"Oh, Meade . . ." Brooke twisted as his hand cupped one of her breasts. He massaged it with a gently squeezing movement. She felt her nipple tighten against the silky fabric of her bra. Meade rolled the pad of his thumb over the bead-hard peak, then flicked it with his nail. A lightning flash of pleasure streaked through her.

Their mouths matched and merged in another kiss. Sweet. Searching. Searing. The connection broke for a gasping instant, then was reestablished with giddy, greedy passion. Brooke nipped lightly at Meade's lower lip. His fingers flexed, kneading her soft, feminine flesh.

He toppled her back onto the sofa, his fingers fumbling for the clasp on the front of her bra. He snapped it open and pushed the flimsy undergarment aside. Beautiful, he thought, drinking in the sight of her.

There was no shame or shyness in Brooke. She relished the hot light she saw flare in the depths of Meade's eyes as he gazed down at her bared breasts. She wanted him to do more than look. She wanted him to taste . . . tease . . . touch . . .

Her skirt was rucked up over her thighs. The denim of his jeans rubbed against the naked skin of her legs. She fumbled for the metal snap at the top of his fly.

Meade slid one hand under the fabric of her tangled skirt and stroked her thigh.

She whispered his name as he touched her, shuddering at the white-hot intensity of the sensation that contact triggered.

The sound of his name on Brooke's lips was like a siren's song. Meade wanted to hear it again and again. He stroked her smooth skin as he pulled her even closer to him.

Brooke moaned, her face flushed. She felt wild . . . wanton . . . like woman incarnate.

She held him to her, boldly running her hands along the length of his muscular back.

This time Meade was the one who cried out.

A moment later, they were one. Brooke gasped at the fullness of his possession. Yet, when he began to move, she reveled in their union, feeling an overwhelming sense of contentment, of wonder.

Ecstasy came like an explosion, shattering everything into countless shimmering pieces. Brooke was locked in Meade's arms, staring deep into his drowningly blue eyes, when she surrendered to it.

Chapter 8

DUSK WAS FALLING. THE SKY, which had been so brilliantly blue just a short time before, was now tinted a purple gray. A playful breeze stirred the warm June air. Meade and Brooke were sitting, as they often did at this hour of the day, in the vine-covered gazebo in the backyard of the house they shared.

Brooke had been enchanted by the latticework structure the first time she'd seen it. She'd asked Meade about it shortly after their initial meeting, and learned that Sebastian Browning had had it built as a birthday present for his wife.

Several days later, she'd come home from work and found Meade out in the gazebo, listening to Mozart and skimming through a stack of the publications that had arrived during his absence. He'd invited her to join him; she'd readily agreed.

The same thing had happened the following evening, only this time Meade had supplemented his invitation to stay and talk with a bottle of Beaujolais.

The next time, Brooke had produced a bottle of Chablis and a pair of cushions to sit on.

A week after they'd made love for the first time, Meade had surprised her with an al fresco supper in the gazebo. They'd eaten at a linen-draped table set with china, crystal, and candles. Like Victorian explorers, Meade had said. And he'd flourished a glass of champagne as he'd toasted the memory of adventurers who'd lived by a code that required they dress for dinner even in the middle of a jungle.

Afterward, with moonlight filtering through the ivy leaves on the gazebo's roof, they'd danced together. Brooke had been intoxicated by the romanticism of it . . .

"So?" Meade asked, draping his right arm around Brooke's shoulders. "What did you *really* think?" He was aware that he was probably sounding like a broken record, but he wanted to be sure . . . very, very sure . . . that the day had gone as well as he thought it had.

Brooke laughed and leaned back, rubbing her cheek against his hand. "I told you in the car coming home, Meade. I think your family is wonderful. I had a marvelous time today."

She was telling the truth. While meeting Meade's immediate relatives—his parents, two sisters, two brothers-in-law, and five nieces and nephews—had been a bit overwhelming, it had also been quite wonderful. She came from a family in which newcomers were acknowledged with proper nods and polite handshakes. She'd spent the day with people who embraced new acquaintances with exuberance. While she knew instinctively that Meade's relatives would have welcomed her for his sake no matter who or what she'd been, she sensed that they'd come to accept her for herself, too.

"You didn't mind discussing roasted rodents at the dinner table?" He toyed with a strand of her hair, twirling it around and around one finger.

"Not at all," Brooke assured him with a quicksilver

smile. "I just wish you could have answered Kevin's question about whether rat meat tastes like chicken."

Meade shook his head. "Honest to God, I don't know where he got the idea I'd eaten rats."

"Well, the fact that he thinks you've done just about *everything* might have something to do with it."

"Mmmm . . ." It was difficult to tell whether he was complimented or concerned by her statement.

Brooke remained silent for a few moments, thinking of the hero worship she'd seen in young Kevin's brown eyes when he'd looked at Meade or spoken about him. And she'd glimpsed the same deeply admiring expression in the hazel eyes of his sister Kathleen's identical twin sons, Joey and Paul Morelli. It had been obvious that all three boys regarded their uncle as some kind of ideal.

He'd seemed to inspired similar feelings in his teenaged nieces, too. Both of them—Alison Morelli and Kevin's sister, Sarah—were at the awkward in-between stage. They'd clearly been excited yet uncertain about the dramatic changes they were undergoing. Brooke had watched how sensitively Meade dealt with their anxieties. He'd behaved in a way that had seemed to assure the girls that even if they felt like ugly ducklings at the moment, they were destined to become beautiful swans very soon.

He'd been so good with them. So very good.

What was it she'd overheard his father say to him weeks ago?

You should have a family . . . of your own!

Francis O'Malley had been right. After spending this day with Meade, Brooke knew that as surely as she'd ever known anything.

Meade began to stroke the curve of Brooke's right shoulder with his thumb. The white gauzy blouse she was wearing had an elasticized neckline. Slowly, he eased the edge of the garment downward.

"You know," he said finally, "I caught the tail end of the

conversation you and my sisters were having in the kitchen—"

"Oh?" she experienced a moment's uneasiness. One of the things she and his sisters had been talking about was his ability with children. She'd realized, with a peculiar sort of shock, that Mary Margaret and Kathleen had taken it upon themselves to make something of a salespitch on their brother's behalf. "A, ah, ploy you picked up from Kevin?"

"Are you going to threaten to paddle me?" he riposted.

"We-e-e-ll . . ." Brooke pretended to contemplate the possibility.

"Don't tell me you're turning kinky, Brooke."

"Kinky?" she repeated delicately, turning her head and giving him a wide-eyed look. "This from a man who once told a ladies' garden club about grow-at-home aphrodisiacs?"

Brooke thought he flushed. But, in the fading light, she couldn't be sure.

"What?" he said. "Who told you *that*?"

"Your sister, Mary Margaret."

"Oh, for Pete's sake!" He forked the fingers of his left hand back through his hair. "What else did she tell—no. Wait. I don't think I want to know."

Brooke waited a beat, then asked mischievously: "Did you?"

"Did I what?"

"Tell a ladies' garden club about . . ."

"No."

"No?"

Meade muttered something. "Well, not exactly," he amended eventually.

"Ah."

"Somebody brought up the subject after my talk. When we were, ah, having tea."

"I see," Brooke said with limpid innocence.

Meade growled. "Look, one woman said she'd heard that *Panax schinseng*—that's ginseng—would give her husband a little, ah, get-up-and-go. I told her some people believe it can have a positive effect on male potency. I also told her that was strictly anecdotal information, not based on validated data or personal experience."

"Oh."

"Disappointed?"

"Not really," Brooke replied. She slanted him a deliberately provocative look. "No personal experience, hmmm?"

His mouth quirked. "Not with ginseng, no."

There was a slight pause. Brooke shifted a little, her left leg bumping Meade's right. She was aware that the right side of her blouse had been slipped off her shoulder.

"Ah . . . you were saying something about your sisters—?" she reminded him after a few moments. It wouldn't really matter if he'd overheard them talking about children, would it? Surely he knew his sisters' sentiments on the subject.

"Oh—yes." He caressed the silky-smooth curve of her bared shoulder slowly. The feel of it was as arousing to him as any mythic aphrodisiac. "I thought I heard the three of you discussing—ah—zombies?"

"Zomb—" she began blankly, then laughed. "Oh. That. Do you remember sending Joey and Paul some Indian necklaces shortly after you got to Brazil?"

Meade frowned for a second, then nodded, not seeing the connection. He'd gotten the beaded ornaments in a trade with a Kamaiura witch doctor. The old man had had a few tricks up his sleeve—so to speak. But the secret of so-called zombification had not been one of them.

"Well," Brooke continued prosaically. "The boys apparently decided the necklaces had the power to turn them into zombies."

Meade regarded her dubiously. "Are you serious?"

"Oh, absolutely. Kathleen said she had two weeks of the

Walking Dead in Brookline before the twins suddenly got bored and announced the evil curse was broken. I told her she'd missed a wonderful opportunity."

"What? A chance to make a little extra cash by selling the story to the tabloids?"

Brooke laughed. "No. As I understand it, every zombie is under the control of a zombie master, right?"

"Voodoo isn't exactly my area of specialization, Brooke."

"Yes, well, according to an article I read, that's the way it supposedly works. The zombie has to obey the zombie master. So, I told Kathleen she should have told Joey and Paul that *she* was a zombie master and then—"

"And then they'd've had to wash their hands and clean up their rooms without a squawk," Meade completed with a roguish grin. "You have a devious mind, sweetheart."

"I try," Brooke said modestly.

There was another pause in their conversation then. Brooke trailed her fingers up the front of his shirt, tracing meandering, meaningless patterns on the knit fabric. Dusk had given way to darkness. A soft night wind rustled the ivy leaves that grew on the outside of the gazebo.

"I noticed you and my mother seemed to find a lot to talk about," Meade remarked after nearly a minute of silence.

Brooke's hand stilled for a moment. Of all the members of Meade's family, she'd been most drawn to his mother. Eleni O'Malley was a small yet sturdy woman with salt-and-pepper hair and snapping brown eyes. She'd seemed almost plain until the first time she'd smiled, and then Brooke had realized she possessed a very special kind of beauty. She was a quiet woman—certainly, as young Kevin had said, much more quiet than her husband. Yet there'd been a strength and serenity in her frequent silences.

"Brooke?" He covered her hand with his own.

"If you meant the conversation we had while you were playing touch football, *you* were the main thing we found to talk about," Brooke answered. Their fingers intertwined.

"Oh?"

"Mmmm . . . she told me you used to run away a lot when you were little."

"True," Meade conceded slowly. "But, I always came home. Besides, it wasn't really running away. It was exploring. I wanted to see what was out there."

"She said that's one reason she and your father decided to let you travel with Professor Browning." Eleni O'Malley had also said something about her and her husband being willing to share their son with a man who had none. "I . . . a lot of parents wouldn't have done that."

"I was lucky," Meade said simply. "I ended up with the right ones."

"She—" Brooke was aware of an odd feeling of surprise. "Your mother used that same word."

"What? Lucky?"

"Yes. She said she was lucky she had you and your sisters." Brooke had been struck by the comment, because most women—most mothers—she knew didn't think in those terms. Those mothers loved their children, of course; but nearly all of them took their existence for granted.

Meade moved his hand from Brooke's shoulder to her cheek and turned her face so he could look directly into it. "Sometimes . . . everything works out," he said softly. And, bending his head, he kissed her.

"Meade?"

"Mmmm?"

"There is *one* thing . . ."

"I know. We-ahhhh." He yawned. "Sorry. We should be going inside. Just give me a few minutes to gather my strength."

Brooke laughed softly and kissed the side of his neck.

She tasted the salty flavor of his sweat. "No. We can stay out here all night if you want. I was . . . I was wondering about something Kevin said this afternoon."

Meade lifted his head slightly and looked down at her. He'd always harbored a wild fantasy about making love to a beautiful woman in the hushed green darkness of a rain forest. Just a short time before, he'd come very close to having the general outline of that fantasy fulfilled.

"Is this something that can and will be held against me?" he inquired huskily, molding the shape of her right side from knee to breast with a bold sweep of his palm. He was conscious that what "strength" he had seemed to have begun gathering of its own accord. He felt as though most of it was congregating between his thighs.

"I—mmmm." Brooke closed her eyes for a moment, giving in to the pleasure that washed over her. When the voluptuous tremor set off by his caress faded, she opened her eyes again. "What . . . what was I saying?"

Meade's teeth showed in a crescent of white. "You were wondering about something Kevin said."

"Oh. Oh, yes. I—who . . . who's Ursula?"

For a moment, Meade pulled a total blank. Then comprehension dawned. "Ah . . . Ursula," he said, suddenly recalling the teasing Brooke had given him earlier on the subject of grow-at-home aphrodisiacs. "Yes. The man she was, ah, involved with, used to live in your apartment."

"Mmmm . . ." Brooke had gathered something like that. "Kevin said he and Paul and Joey used to come over and visit her."

"Oh, sure. Ursula loved the attention."

"He said they used to visit her in *your* apartment."

"Jealous?"

Brooke hesitated. Was she—? Yes. She was. Of course, she was! Oh, she'd always known there had been women in Meade's life before she'd entered it. And she'd made her peace with that knowledge . . . more or less. But there was something *different* about this Ursula. Kevin had positively beamed when he'd referred to her.

"I'm just . . . curious, Meade," she said finally. "Kevin seemed to think she was something special."

"He was one of her biggest fans. Didn't even mind that she liked to squeeze."

Brooke blinked. "Squeeze—?"

"Ursula was—well, actually, she was like you in a lot of ways, Brooke."

"Like me?" This was the last thing she'd expected—or wanted—to hear.

"Mmmm-hmm. She was very, ah, supple." He reached downward . . .

"Supple." Brooke half said, half swallowed the word as she felt the caress of Meade's hand.

"Sinuous." His pronunciation of the word was slow. The stroke of his fingers was even slower.

"Sin—sinuous."

"Sleek."

"S-sleek?"

"She loved to be touched . . ."

Brooke had to bite her lip to keep from moaning at the pleasure his fondling was stirring in her.

"Alison and Sarah thought she was slimy." Meade lowered his voice as he imparted the unfortunate news.

"What—?" Brooke tilted her head back, clutching at his upper arms.

"She wasn't, of course." He kissed the underside of her jaw. "However, she *was* cold-blooded."

"C-cold—" Brooke tried to fit this with the rest of his description. It was a bit like piecing together a jigsaw puzzle during an earthquake. "You . . . ah-ah—Meade! You m-make her sound like a—a—snake!"

He grinned wickedly. "That's Ursula."

* * *

Later—a long time later—Brooke told Meade she was going to find a way to get back at him.

She sensed that the fact that she was smiling like a bliss-sated idiot when she said it undercut the persuasiveness of her threat.

Little Jonathan Wilding was christened late the following afternoon. In Brooke's opinion, he behaved himself beautifully. She felt his one small lapse in decorum—an indignant howl of protest at a particularly solemn moment—was perfectly understandable and therefore quite excusable.

"I suppose you each think you'd react with perfect aplomb if someone woke you out of a sound sleep by pouring water on your head?" Brooke inquired of Meade and Ethan Wilding at the small at-home reception after the ceremony. The two men had been trading joking comments about Jonathan's prodigious lung power.

"Didn't you once do that to me in college?" Meade asked Ethan.

"What? Wake you out of a sound sleep by pouring water on your head?" Ethan seemed to reflect back. "You know, I believe I did. I think it was during final exam week our first semester. You'd pulled two all-nighters and I was trying to get you up for an English lit test."

"And? Did I react with perfect aplomb?"

"Well, as I remember, Meade, you damned near broke my nose."

Meade made a dismissive gesture. "But I didn't yell."

"Nnnnn-no," Ethan said slowly, as though reviewing the sequence of events in his mind. "I seem to recall that I was the one doing the yelling."

"Like father, like son," Meade declared.

"Oh, honestly!" Brooke tried not to laugh.

"Here he is, the star of the show," Jazz announced, materializing with her son in her arms.

"What happened to his coronation outfit?" Meade asked, surveying his new godson. He stroked the baby's pudgy cheeks with one knuckle. Despite his irreverent tone, Brooke could tell that his touch was exquisitely gentle.

"Do you mean his christening gown, you Greco-Hibernian savage?" Ethan challenged with mock, Boston Brahmin loftiness.

"Whatever. The imperial frou-frou." Meade gave Brooke a quick wink. "All that white stuff you had Jonathan trussed up in before."

"You're talking about a Wilding family tradition, Meade," Jazz said with a hint of severity. "Ethan wore it once, you know."

"Oh, really? Ethan in heirloom lace?" Meade raised his brows. His voice implied he'd like to see pictures of that. Possibly for purposes of blackmail.

"Thanks, love," Ethan said to his wife, his tone martini dry.

"You're welcome," she responded with a flirtatious wink. Then she looked at Brooke. "Would you like to hold him again?"

"Oh, yes—" Brooke accepted the baby carefully, cradling his sleeping body against her. She brushed at his satin-fluff eruption of red-gold hair with one finger. Suddenly, his finely lashed lids opened to reveal huge blue eyes. He stared at her unblinkingly for a second, then his sleep-flushed features crinkled into a giant yawn. She smiled down at him and murmured his name in a tender tone.

"I suppose you're going to have your firstborn decked out in beads and feathers and dunked in the Amazon River?" Ethan asked Meade, nudging him in the ribs.

Meade was watching Brooke. Her pale hair was swept up and off her face. To his eyes, the pure line of her downbent profile was achingly beautiful. The curve of her soft, ripe lips was as warmly lovely as a summer sunrise.

Yes, he thought. *Oh, yes.*

"Could be," he said to his friend.

Brooke was conscious of a vague feeling of uneasiness as she and Meade drove home from the christening. They talked very little. He seemed oddly withdrawn—even tense—to her. After one or two attempts at drawing him into a conversation, Brooke lapsed into silence. It was probably just as well, she told herself. If his emotions were uncharacteristically submerged, hers were unusually close to the surface. Light chitchat was not very appealing to her.

"I—ah—I finished reading the draft for your lecture," Brooke volunteered a bit tentatively when they entered the house. "Do you want to come up—?"

"Sure," Meade accepted with a nod, thrusting his hands into the pockets of his trousers. "Just let me get out of this suit."

"Okay," she agreed.

Her phone started to ring the instant she got her door open. She dashed into the kitchen to answer it.

"Hello?"

"Brooke?"

"Oh, hello, Mother," she said, not particularly surprised. Her mother called nearly every weekend. Brooke slipped her shoes off and wiggled her toes.

"Where have you been, dear? I've been calling for hours."

"I was at a christening. Remember? I told you I'd been asked to be a godmother?"

"Oh . . . oh, yes. The baby you helped deliver."

"That's right."

"You know, Brooke, I've thought about that. It must have been terribly hard for you."

Brooke pulled off one of the gold and jade drop earrings she was wearing, trying not to resent her mother's tone.

Compassion she could accept; pity, no. Her mother's pity—poor Brooke, poor barren Brooke—had been one reason she'd left Connecticut and come to Boston.

"What must have been terribly hard for me? Helping deliver Jonathan or being his godmother?" Brooke realized she was probably being unfair, but she couldn't help it.

"Well . . . both, I suppose."

"I wasn't alone, Mother."

"You're talking about this anthropologist you're living with."

"Ethnobotanist." Brooke decided not to argue over the phrase *living with*. She and Meade had no formal commitment, no articulated arrangement; but she did "live with" him . . .

"Yes . . . yes. Does he know about you, dear? About your . . . problem?"

Brooke's fingers tightened around the telephone. "No. I—it's never come up. He and I—no."

"He's one of these men who doesn't want children?"

"Mother—" She thought of Meade with his nieces and nephews. With little Jonathan. She thought of what his sisters had said to her the day before. Of what she'd overheard his father say to him . . .

"It makes a difference, dear—"

"I know it makes a difference!" Brooke snapped. "Mother, I don't want to talk about it, all right? Please. I don't want to talk about it!"

There was a long silence from the other end.

"Fine," her mother said eventually. "We won't talk about it. I didn't intend to upset you."

Brooke sighed. "I know, Mother. I know. I didn't mean to be rude. It's just—oh, never mind. Did you have a reason for calling?"

There was another silence.

"Mother?"

"Well, I'm not sure I should say anything now."

Brooke pulled off her other earring and dropped it on the kitchen counter along with the first one. "Of course, you should," she replied, instinctively bracing herself.

"Actually—your sister is the one who told me."

"What is it, Mother?"

"She . . . she thought you should hear it from one of us. It's about Peter."

Brooke swallowed and let a few seconds go by.

"What about . . . him?" she asked at last. She'd never told her mother the whole truth about the breakup of her marriage. This was partly because it had never been easy for her, even under the best of circumstances, to talk with her mother about sex and the intimate details of male-female relations. It was also because the whole truth—or, what she'd thought was the whole truth—had been too humiliating, too hurtful, for her to confide to anyone.

"His wife is expecting, dear."

The past rose up and stabbed Brooke in the heart. She closed her eyes. "Which proves, conclusively, that it really was my fault he and I didn't have any children, right?" she responded bitterly. "Peter must be very, very happy."

"Brooke—"

Why? You want to know why, Brooke? Because I'm a man and I can't get what I want—what I need—from you! You can't give me a son and you can't give me much satisfaction, either! You're not just infertile—you're frigid too!

Half-right. Peter had only been half-right. Brooke knew that now. She *wasn't* frigid.

But she was . . .

"Brooke?"

"I—I appreciate your telling me this, Mother," Brooke said politely. "But, ah, I—I've got to go now, all right?"

"Well—"

"Give my love to Dad. I'll talk to you soon."

"Are you all—"

"I'm fine, Mother. Really. I do have to say good-bye,

though. I'm expecting someone any second."

"Well . . . if you're sure . . ."

"I am. Good-bye, Mother."

"Good-bye, Brooke."

Brooke hung up the phone. She was trembling.

"Brooke?"

The trembling stopped. It was Meade's voice, coming from her living room.

"In—I'm in the kitchen," she managed to get out.

Meade walked in a moment later. The sight of him hit Brooke so hard, she was amazed her knees didn't buckle.

"I—I thought you were going to change," she said. He was still in the elegant navy suit he'd worn to the christening. The same suit he'd had on the second time she'd seen him, when he'd brought her flowers.

Meade shook his head. "I . . . decided what I want to say requires a touch of formality," he told her, his expression very serious.

Some instinct made her grope for the edge of the counter.

"What . . . what is it you want to say?" she asked.

"Marry me, Brooke."

Chapter 9

MARRY ME, BROOKE.

Three words. Three simple words.

It seemed to Brooke that everything stopped when she heard them—including her heart.

For an instant, all she knew was joy. She felt incandescent with it.

But only for an instant.

Then her heart started beating again. Brooke reminded herself to breathe.

"M-marry you?" she repeated in a small voice. She'd never, ever dreamed—

Oh, yes. Oh, yes, she had. She knew she had.

How many times had she studied Meade—secretly, when he was sleeping, or covertly, when they were in a crowd of people—and imagined what it would be like to spend the rest of her life with him? How many times had she lain in his arms and fantasized about a future that could never be hers?

But *he'd* never said, never hinted—

Not for the first time, Meade seemed to divine the direction of her thoughts.

"I know," he said, gesturing as though to indicate that he was surrendering to some force far greater than himself. Brooke stared at his hands, at the faintly callused palms and long, strong fingers. She remembered with a searingly sweet sense of yearning how it felt to have them touching her. "I know, I should have led up to this with a little more finesse," he elaborated. "Forgive me, sweetheart? I've never done—I've never felt—" He shook his head, his eyes brilliant. "Marry me. Please. Marry me."

There was a moment of silence. Brooke finally broke it with a single word.

"Why?"

Meade seemed puzzled for an instant, as though not quite believing he'd heard her question correctly. Brooke watched as a small frown briefly pleated the skin between his dark brows. Then, abruptly, his expression cleared.

"Because I love you," he replied with passionate simplicity. "I've never said that, have I? God knows, I should have. I love you, Brooke. I want us to make a life together. A *family* together. We can have everything, sweetheart—"

He moved to her then, and put his arms around her, gathering her against him with infinite gentleness. Brooke felt the press of his lips against her temple, the stir of his breath through the fine tendrils at her hairline.

A life together, he'd said. A *family.*

"I've really taken you by surprise, haven't I?" he murmured with rueful tenderness. Brooke thought she heard a thread of something else—could it be uncertainty?—in his question as well. "I'm sorry. I wanted to do this—coming home from the christening, coming up the stairs, I kept rehearsing what I should say and how I should say it. I was ready to go down on one knee. But, instead, I walked in and blurted everything out—"

Brooke turned her face up to look at him. "You decided

. . . you decided at the christening?" she asked. "That's when—?"

Meade stroked his thumbs against the small of her back.. His hands weren't quite steady. Neither was his voice when he responded.

"It wasn't so much 'deciding' as . . . *knowing*," he told her. "I think, deep down, I've known from the very beginning that you were the one . . . the woman I'd always hoped to find but never completely believed existed. But today, at the christening, seeing you with Jonathan—it was like a revelation, Brooke. The way you were holding him, caring for him. Do you have any idea how beautiful you looked? I kept thinking what it would've been like if Jonathan had been ours. I kept imagining—Lord, I almost asked you right then and there."

"Meade—"

"And yesterday, with my family—" He dipped his head and brushed his lips across hers. "Marry me," he urged softly, planting butterfly-light kisses on each corner of her mouth. Then he began nuzzling a tantalizing trail down the side of her neck. Brooke heard herself making a murmuring sound in response.

Marry me, was what he said.

Be my wife . . . have my children, was what he really meant.

She took a deep breath, trying to steel herself against the effect of his seductive caress. The air she inhaled seemed to burn her lungs like an acid mist.

"I can't," she whispered rawly.

She had the impression that it was her tone, not her words, that reached him. Meade lifted his head abruptly and looked down at her. His hands, which had been stroking up her spine, stilled.

"What?" he asked.

"I can't . . . marry you, Meade."

He went pale beneath his tan and his features tautened as though she'd struck him.

"Why not?"

"Because . . ." She should tell him. She should tell him, now.

And if she did?

Meade wouldn't reject her the way Peter had done. Instinctively, she knew that. No, what he'd do would, in many ways, be worse.

He'd tell her that it didn't matter. That he loved her and wanted to marry her anyway. That having children wasn't truly important to him. He would tell her all these things and he might even make himself believe them . . . for a while.

But she wouldn't believe them.

Brooke understood the pain of longing for children and not being able to have them. She could not deliberately inflict that pain on anyone—much less the man she loved. And she did love Meade O'Malley. If she had never fully admitted that to herself before, she admitted it now. She'd tumbled into love with him the first time she'd seen him.

"Brooke?"

"No, Meade," she said, shaking her head once. "I can't."

"'Can't' isn't a reason!" His previous pallor had given way to a flush of frustration. Angry blood darkened the ridges of his cheekbones. The tension she'd sensed in him earlier was uncoiling like a whip.

"Please—"

"Please, *what*?" he demanded, his eyes shooting sapphire sparks. "Do you love me, Brooke?"

She almost broke down at the question. "Yes, I love you!" Dear God, she loved him more than she believed it was possible for her to love another person.

She saw the muscles in his lean jaw clench and unclench. "You love me," he repeated tautly. "But not enough to marry me. Is that it?"

Brooke averted her head for a second, not wanting to see the expression on his face. For some reason she couldn't explain, her mind flashed back to the night she'd tried to tell him the full truth about herself and her marriage and he'd stopped her.

What could she say to him? That she loved him *too* much to marry him?

Meade hooked two fingers under her chin and forced her to look at him.

"Is that it?" he asked harshly. "You love me enough to be my lover, but not enough to be my wife? You love me enough to share my bed, but not my life?"

"Meade—"

He let go of her and took a step back. His hands were balled into fists. "Dammit, tell me why, Brooke!"

"I can't!"

"You mean, you won't."

Desperate, Brooke said the first thing that came into her head.

"Meade, I've been married before—" she began, then stopped as she saw his pupils dilate with shock.

"You think being married to me would be like that?" he asked in a terrible voice. He uttered a single, savage obscenity, then turned on his heel.

He was out of the kitchen before Brooke even began to accept what had just happened. Out of her apartment before her pain-numbed brain forced her emotionally paralyzed body to move.

"Meade!" she cried. Oh, God. Oh, God—what had she done?

Somehow, she stumbled out onto the second-floor landing. Meade was already down the stairs and at the front door.

"Meade!" This time she could barely get his name out.

He yanked open the door.

"Wh-where are you going?"

He checked himself for an instant, but didn't turn around.

"Away from here," was all he said.

He slammed the door on his way out. It seemed to Brooke that the entire house rocked with the violence of it.

A few moments later, she heard him drive away.

Meade did not come back that night.

Brooke kept a lonely vigil on the stairs . . . waiting . . . waiting.

In the beginning, it was a relief to be able to weep. She cried in an effort to purge the pain and the guilt, the anger and the grief. It helped a little. But, after several hours, she found she had no tears left to shed. She felt achingly, agonizingly empty.

The house, without Meade's presence, felt the same way.

She kept seeing the look on his face when he'd asked her if she thought being married to him would be like being married to Peter.

She kept hearing the pain in his voice.

She stared at the front door, remembering the way he'd slammed it when he left.

Where are you going?

Away from here.

He had to come back.

If he didn't come back . . . she'd go out and find him.

The next morning, after much internal debate, Brooke made up her mind to go to work. Maybe, she told herself, just maybe, Meade would turn up at WIWE.

She did what she could to repair the ravages of a sleepless, tear-filled night. But, no matter how much makeup she put on, the face in her bathroom mirror remained red-eyed and drawn. She finally threw down the tube of concealing cream she was attempting to smooth on over the marks of strain and turned away from her reflection.

Where are you going?

Away from here.

She tried not to think about the fact that for Achimedes Xavier O'Malley, "away" could mean anywhere in the world. *Anywhere.*

She tried not to think about it . . . but she still let herself into his apartment to check that his passport was in his desk. He'd gotten it out and showed it to her one evening when they'd been talking about his travels, so she knew exactly where to look to find it.

It was there, its gold-embossed blue cover as dog-eared as she recalled and its finger-smudged pages still full of exotic-looking immigration stamps and health certifications. She touched the document as though she were touching the man it belonged to.

A note, she decided. She should leave a note in case Meade returned while she was away. With trembling fingers, she found pen and paper. She wrote his name, followed by three sentences, then signed her own name at the bottom.

Please, she prayed, rereading what she'd written. Oh, please.

The phone on his desk rang, startling her so badly she jumped. She snatched up the receiver.

"H-Hello?" Brooke held her breath.

"Hello?" a bright, boyish voice responded.

Brooke exhaled heavily. "Kevin."

"Miss Livingstone?" Kevin sounded surprised yet pleased.

"Yes . . . that's right."

"How come you're talking on Uncle Meade's phone?"

"I, ah, heard it ringing and picked it up."

There was a fractional pause. "Do you have the same

phone number as him? 'Cuz you're living in the same house, I mean?"

"No, Kevin, I don't."

"Oh. I thought maybe—huh? Just a second, okay?" There were some fumbling sounds from his end of the line. "—not being a pest, Sarah! Uncle Meade said I could call him up. Uh-huh, he did. And Mom said it was okay, too. What? I'm talking to Miss Livingstone. Huh? No! Get out! You never let me—oh, yeah, yeah. Yeah, yeah." More fumbling noises. "Miss Livingstone?"

"I'm still here, Kevin."

"That was my dumb sister Sarah. She says hi."

"Please say hi back."

"Okay. *If* I'm still talking to her, that is. You know on Saturday, Uncle Meade told me and Joey and Paul we should be special nice to Sarah and Alison 'cuz they're going through this, um, weird girl stuff? Well, boy, I don't know. I mean, Uncle Meade said the way they are is normal but . . ." Brooke could practically see him wrinkling his freckled nose in disdain. "Anyway, can I talk to Uncle Meade?"

Brooke knew the question had been inevitable since the moment she'd first heard the boy's voice. That didn't make hearing it any easier.

"I—he's not here right now, Kevin."

"Oh? How come?"

"He went out."

"To run? He does that sometimes in the—"

"No, not to run," Brooke interrupted quickly. Then something occurred to her. "Did . . . did you two have plans for today?"

"Nah," Kevin answered a bit glumly. "But he said maybe we could hang out together this week. 'Cept not on Wednesday. That's when me and Dad are going to see the Red Sox play. Dad and me have these guys' nights out, you know? Just him and me. No Sarah. 'Cuz I think she's making him go nuts, too, only he can't say it 'cuz he might give her one of those psycho-complex things." The boy heaved a sigh. "Rats. I really wanted to talk to Uncle Meade. Ummm, can you tell him I called? When he comes back, I mean. Please?"

"Well, I'm going off to work right now, Kevin," Brooke answered, trying to keep her voice steady. "But, I'll leave him a message—all right?"

"Yeah, all right." He accepted the idea with enthusiasm. "That'd be really good. Say he should call me up, okay? Thanks."

"You're welcome."

"Uh—Miss Livingstone?"

"Yes, Kevin?"

"Are you okay? You sound kind of funny."

Brooke discovered that the reservoir of tears she thought she'd drained was not quite empty. She wiped her fingers under her eyes.

"I'm fine," she lied, and hoped that she sounded more convincing than she had the last time she'd said those words in Meade's apartment.

Meade did not turn up at the Wilding Institute for World Exploration that day. But a number of his colleagues did. Brooke tried, as discreetly as she could, to ascertain whether any of them had seen Meade since the previous evening. None of them had.

"Meade O'Malley?" one of them had replied with a faintly admiring smile and a faintly exasperated shrug. "I didn't even realize he was back from Brazil until the other day when somebody mentioned it in Elsie's Deli. I swear, he gets around like a flock of migratory geese—if you overlook the fact that migratory geese follow some kind of pattern. With Meade . . . well, did you ever hear about the time—?"

Brooke had heard. From several people. The first three times, she hadn't believed it. Now, she did.

She called Meade's apartment—and his departmental office—over and over during the day. Each time, she listened to the ringing on the other end go on and on and on. There was never any answer.

Where are you going?

Away from here.

"Away from me . . ." she muttered miserably as she hung up the phone after what must have been her dozenth call to the house. It was now late afternoon. Nearly twenty-four hours had elapsed since she'd seen Meade.

She raised her head, staring up at the stuffed vulture that hung from the ceiling. The ominous-looking example of some anonymous taxidermist's art stared back with glassy eyes, swaying ever so slightly.

What if something had happened to him? she asked herself, chewing her bottom lip. What if he'd been . . . hurt? What if he was somewhere—

"Brooke?"

She started. Daniel Quincy stood in the doorway to her office, holding a sheaf of papers.

"Yes, Mr. Quincy?" she questioned anxiously. She knew he'd noted her pale face and puffy eyes when she'd come in that morning. But, aside from a mild comment about the day's pollen count, he'd refrained from saying anything about them. She'd been grateful for his tact.

The silver-haired man entered and placed the papers on Brooke's desk. "Meade's preliminary draft on the Xingu Basin," he explained. "I'd like two copies, when you have a few moments."

"Of course." Brooke rose to her feet.

"Tell me, did you have a hand in preparing this?"

"Well—" She wasn't quite certain what he meant. "Meade did ask me to read over it. I suggested a few changes, that's all."

"Mmmm. I thought I detected your deft editorial influence."

The compliment surprised and touched her. "Thank you."

"Not at all." He smiled just a little as though savoring a pleasant thought. "Gaby Browning used to edit Sebastian's work, I remember. And thank the Lord for that. The man was utterly brilliant in his field, of course. But, to be brutally frank, he couldn't parse a sentence with a machete. He was also the most atrocious speller I've ever encountered." With that, he turned away to make his exit.

Brooke picked up the papers and clutched them against her, feeling her throat work. She knew the institute's executive director well enough to recognize that his last comments had been more than a casual reminiscence. "Mr.—Mr. Quincy?" she asked.

Her employer looked back at her questioningly. "Yes?"

"Have you . . . have you heard from Meade today?"

Daniel Quincy frowned slightly, his bushy silver brows knitting together. "No, my dear, I haven't," he answered. "I'm sorry. But . . . I'm certain he'll be in touch."

The house was empty when Brooke arrived home. The two notes she'd left Meade were still taped to the door of his apartment, obviously untouched and unread.

She spent several hours sitting out in the gazebo, watching the day dissolve into night, contemplating what she should do. The fear that something might have happened to Meade gnawed at her unmercifully. She had reached the point where all she wanted was to know that he was safe.

Well, not *all* . . . but she would settle for that knowledge as a start.

Dear heaven, she loved him so much! She'd tried to do what was best. She had! But, instead . . .

Brooke wrapped her arms around herself, feeling chilled

despite the balmy evening weather. It had gone wrong. So terribly wrong. She'd do anything—*anything*—to set it right.

Finally, she got up and called Meade's mother.

Eleni O'Malley said she had not seen nor heard from her son since he'd kissed her good-bye on Saturday.

What little sleep Brooke got that night she got in Meade's bed, hugging a pillow that carried the scent of his skin.

"Do you . . . do you know where Meade is?" Brooke asked Eleni O'Malley with desperate directness shortly after noon the following day. Meade's mother had appeared at her office about fifteen minutes earlier and invited her to lunch. Brooke had resisted; Eleni had insisted.

The older woman unfolded a paper napkin and placed it on her lap. "No," she said simply. "Which, I will tell you honestly, is not unusual."

Brooke bit the inside of her lip and glanced down for a moment. Eleni had taken her to a small, family-style restaurant. The proprietor—"a cousin," she'd explained—had welcomed them with literally opened arms. Eleni and the man had had a rapid conversation in Greek. Afterward, they'd been shown to a relatively quiet corner booth near the back. A waitress had materialized within moments, delivering wine and bread and some stuffed grape leaves, then faded away and not returned.

Brooke raised her head and looked across the table. "Would you tell me if you did know, Mrs. O'Malley?"she questioned.

There was extraordinary sympathy in Meade's mother's dark eyes. "Yes," she responded after a moment, then lifted her brows in a way that reminded Brooke of Meade. "I thought we agreed you would call me 'Eleni.'"

Brooke nodded distractedly. There was a basket of rolls

on the table. She reached for one and began breaking it into pieces.

"I—I'm so afraid something's happened to him... Eleni," she confessed tautly. "If anything—it would be *my* fault—"

Eleni reached across the table and stopped Brooke's unthinking destruction of the roll. "It takes two people to make a quarrel," she observed quietly. She paused while Brooke drew a ragged breath. "I know you very carefully said 'misunderstanding' last night, Brooke. But I think it was much more than that."

Brooke let the crumbled remains of the roll slip through her fingers. The affinity she'd felt for Eleni O'Malley from the first moments of their first meeting reasserted itself.

"He... Meade asked me to marry him," she said at last.

There was no hint of surprise on Eleni's olive-toned face. "And?" she prompted gently.

"And I said no."

The older woman's brows came together. "You don't love him?"

It was not an accusation, but Brooke reacted defensively. "Of course I love him!" she said fiercely, feeling the needle prick of tears at the corners of her eyes. She blinked rapidly, not wanting to cry. "I do love him," she repeated in a softer but no less intense voice. "I love him so m-much..."

"Shhh... shhh..." The sound was soothing.

Brooke picked up a napkin and wiped at her eyes. "I—I'm s-sorry," she faltered.

Eleni shook her head. "You feel strongly. That's nothing to apologize for. Love... being able to love is a blessing, Brooke. Not an unmixed one. Sometimes it's a heavy gift to bear. But, even when it is—it's a rare burden. Please. Can you—*will* you tell me why you won't marry my son?"

Brooke crumpled up the napkin into a tight little ball and dropped it on the tabletop along with a pile of mangled roll pieces. "Because I can't give him what he wants," she said starkly.

What she saw in Eleni O'Malley's face then *was* surprise—even shock. Under different circumstances, the older woman's expression would have been almost amusing.

"Brooke . . ." Meade's mother began, obviously searching for words. "Brooke, I saw you with my son. I saw the way he looked at you, the way you looked at him. For three weeks before I met you I heard the way he spoke of you. And I knew that at long last—I think we all knew . . ." She leaned forward. "What could Meade want that you can't give him? That you *haven't* given him?"

Brooke felt herself flush, then go pale. How could she answer such a question?

Never be sorry about telling the truth.

Brooke remembered when Meade had said those words to her. And she remembered the way they'd come to her the night they'd first made love. She hadn't been sorry that night . . .

"I can't give your son a child, Eleni," she said quietly. "I can't . . . I can't have children."

The older woman flinched, but stayed silent.

"That's one of the reasons my first marriage broke up," Brooke went on levelly, then hesitated. "You—you *did* know I was married before?" she asked. Her divorce was one subject Francis O'Malley hadn't broached the first day they'd met.

Eleni nodded slowly. Her normally mellifluous voice was slightly muffled when she spoke: "Yes. I knew. Meade told Francis—oh, weeks ago it must be now. And Francis told me, of course. But Meade didn't say anything—"

"He couldn't. He didn't—he doesn't—know. There were . . . there were other problems with my marriage to Peter. Meade understood those. In a way, I think he understood them better than I did. But all those problems . . ."

She shook her head. "Not being able to get pregnant is such a personal kind of failure. Having a baby is supposed to be so natural. The most natural thing in the world. And when you find out that that natural thing is impossible . . ."

She looked at Meade's mother. The surprise had gone from the other woman's face. In its place were understanding and compassion and another emotion Brooke couldn't decipher.

"Meade wants children," she continued after a moment. "He told me."

"He wants you, too," Eleni returned. "He told you that when he asked you to marry him."

"But he didn't know I couldn't have—"

"You think he wouldn't have asked if he had?" It was a challenge.

"I—"

"What if it was the other way around, Brooke? What if you knew Meade couldn't give you the children you wanted and he asked you to marry him—would you refuse?"

Brooke went very still.

Oh, God, she thought. What have I done—

"No . . ." she said. It was absolute. Unconditional. *"No."*

It was like an explosion in her heart and mind. Brooke suddenly saw what she'd done to herself—what she'd done to Meade. She'd been afraid of Meade's pity because self-pity was something she'd been wallowing in for a long, long time. And she'd been afraid of his rejection because, deep down, she doubted her own worth . . . she felt she *deserved* rejection.

She'd told herself she "accepted" what she was . . . and what she wasn't. She hadn't accepted anything! She'd embraced her inability to have a baby like a hair shirt. She'd allowed it to define and limit her life. She'd been obsessed by it!

She looked at Meade's mother. "Oh . . . oh, Eleni . . ."

"I know," the older woman said gently. "I know."

Brooke believed her. She didn't understand why, but she did. "How—?" she started.

"It's not important now," came the firm answer. "What's important is that *you* know."

"I know I have to find Meade. I have to—I have to tell him. To make him understand . . ." Brooke was ready to tell Meade everything. The whole truth. From beginning to end. And she would pray that in doing so, they could start anew . . . together.

Eleni O'Malley smiled, transforming her entire face. "You will," she assured Brooke. Then her eyes took on a vibrant sparkle. "But first, you'll have some lunch. No moussaka. It's terrible here."

For the first time in nearly two days, Brooke laughed.

Meade O'Malley sat in the living room of his apartment staring at one of the notes he'd found taped to his door when he'd come in about thirty minutes before.

"Meade—" it began. "Forgive me. Please stay. I love you."

It was signed: "Brooke."

He'd been half out of his mind with hurt and anger and confusion when he slammed out of the house two days before. He hadn't known where he was going when he got into his car; and, in all truth, he hadn't given a damn.

He'd driven around for a few hours and eventually wound up at Logan Airport. He'd stayed there most of the night. Meade knew he'd garnered more than a few questioning glances but, again, he hadn't given a damn.

Around dawn, he'd driven to the Botanical Museum back in Cambridge. The overnight security guard, a man who'd been on the job as long as Meade could remember, had been happy to let him in.

He'd gone to the fourth floor, to a broom closet–sized

office that had once been Sebastian Browning's. His mentor and friend had practically lived in the place during the year following his return to Boston and the news that Gabrielle was dead.

The professor had done almost no work for those twelve months. He'd refused to discuss anything about the field study he'd been engaged in at the time of his wife's death. Meade had finally confronted him, asking what he did every day in that small, cell-like space.

"I sit and I ask why," had been Sebastian Browning's reply.

And that had been what Meade had spent most of the past thirty-six hours doing. Ultimately, he'd come to the conclusion that the answer to the question he kept asking over and over and over wasn't going to be found where he was.

So, he'd gone back to the house he'd stormed out of two days before. He'd gone back to the terribly empty house and he'd waited for the woman who could fill it . . . and his arms . . . and his heart.

Forgive me.

Anything. He'd forgive her anything. And he hoped she'd do the same for him.

Please stay.

He had no intention of leaving. And no intention of letting her go, either.

I love you.

Oh, sweet heaven, let that be true. It wasn't that nothing else mattered; it was simply that nothing else mattered as much.

Afterward, when he sought a rational explanation for what he did when he heard Brooke's car pull into the drive, Meade failed to come up with one. He simply did it.

* * *

Drums . . . mimicking the rhythmic beat of the human heart.

Flutes . . . piping an oddly atonal yet insinuating melody that seemed designed to arouse the singing of the human bloodstream.

And singing. Was someone singing?

Brooke heard the hauntingly primitive music before she got the front door unlocked. Once she actually opened the door and stepped into the house, she found herself trembling in response to its seductive message.

Meade's door was closed.

She crossed to it and knocked. Once. Twi—

The door opened and Brooke saw the man she loved. A man with eyes the color of a sun-lit sea.

He opened his arms to her.

Archimedes Xavier O'Malley was home . . . and so was she.

Chapter 10

"I HAVE SOMETHING I HAVE to tell you," Brooke said many delirious minutes later. The tape that had been playing had run out. Exactly when, she didn't know. It didn't matter. The music was inside her now, playing in her brain and body.

Somehow—she had no idea how it had been accomplished—they'd gotten from his front door to one of his living room sofas. She could see that the route they'd taken had been less than direct. Their erratic course was clearly marked by her shoes, his tie, her shoulder bag, his suit jacket, and three-quarters of the bobby pins that had been holding her workday chignon in place.

Meade shifted her within the circle of his arms so he could look directly into her face. He could see the smudges of exhaustion and anxiety beneath her eyes. Her pale, poreless skin seemed more tightly stretched over her cheekbones than he remembered. And there were new shadows and hollows around her finely drawn features.

The past two days had left their mark on her, and he was sorry for it.

Yet, for all the signs of stress and strain and sleeplessness, Meade thought he detected a new strength . . . a new certainty in Brooke. It was as though the contradictions he'd sensed in her the first time they'd met had been brought together and reconciled.

And now, after a reunion of kisses and caresses that had shaken him to the very depths of his soul, she said she had something she had to tell him . . .

"What is it?" he questioned, his voice low and deep.

Brooke took a deep breath. "First, I *do* love you, Meade. I love you with all my heart. With all my . . . everything. And what I did Sunday was done out of love. A—a misguided kind of love," she added swiftly, seeing his eyes darken. "I know that now, Meade. What I did Sunday was as misguided as what I did the first time we made love together."

"Brooke—"

She shook her head and pressed a finger to his lips. "No, please. Let me go on. I love you, Meade. And—and, despite what I said, I do want to make a life with you."

"Then why did you—" No. Meade choked off the question. He knew he had to let Brooke do this in her own way, at her own speed.

Go slowly.

That was what she'd asked of him almost from the very beginning. He hadn't gone slowly on Sunday. He'd let himself be swept away by the force of his own emotions. It had been a mistake. A terrible mistake. It was not one he wanted to repeat.

Brooke gazed into Meade's compelling face for several long moments. He looked weary. The lines that fanned out from the corners of his eyes and bracketed his mouth were etched more deeply than she recalled, and there was tension in the set of his sensually shaped lips. Beard stubble darkened his chin and jaw.

He'd told her how he'd spent the past two days. In the

wake of her wild relief at seeing him safe had come a brief surge of anger. She'd demanded to know where he'd gone, and he'd told her. Though his answer had been brief, she'd known that he'd suffered the same kind of hell she had.

Brooke took no satisfaction from this knowledge. She would have spared him the hurt if she could have. But she hadn't been able to. She could only hope that the pain was over and done with.

She touched Meade's lean, tanned cheek. He turned his head, blue eyes very bright, and pressed his lips against the center of her palm. It was as though he'd kissed her very core.

It was several seconds before she could begin to speak. And several more before her voice was entirely steady.

"When you asked me to marry you," she said, "you told me you wanted us to have a family. You said . . . you said seeing me with Jonathan was what made you—that you kept thinking what it would've been like if he were ours." She tilted her chin slightly, her unpinned hair rippling back like cornsilk. She looked deep into his eyes. "I can't give you a family. I can't have children, Meade."

"You can't—" He couldn't believe—he couldn't believe *that* was why she'd refused to marry him. Good God, did she think—

And then his mind replayed everything she'd said, and the memory of how he'd proposed flooded in. Of course, she thought! Nearly every other word out of his mouth on Sunday had been a reference to children! Even before he'd told her he loved her, he'd talked about children. And he had no doubt that his well-meaning family had sounded a similar theme on Saturday.

Brooke saw the change in his expression and knew he'd begun to blame himself. She couldn't let him do that. The time for blaming—if there'd ever been one—was over.

"Meade, no." Again, she stroked his cheek. "If you want children, you should have them. You *should* be a father. You're so wonderful with Kevin and the twins and the two girls. You have—you have a gift for loving, for caring."

"But—"

"I know what it's like to want children and not be able to have them. I've known the emptiness . . . the anger . . . the envy. I'm trying to let go of those feelings, Meade. I don't want them twisting my life up anymore. But, most of all, I don't . . . I don't want you to know those feelings."

"Oh, Brooke, sweetheart—"

From there, Brooke went on to tell him the story of her marriage to Peter. She faltered once or twice, but she told him everything. She held nothing back, including the realizations she'd come to that afternoon while talking with his mother.

"That first night . . ." He glanced toward one of the tables by the fireplace. "My God, that first night it was the fertility statue that upset you, wasn't it? That's why you left."

Brooke nodded once. "That was part of it," she conceded. "And part of it was being so confused by my reaction to you. You made me feel—you made me feel things I didn't know I was capable of feeling."

"And when you came to help Jazz in the labor room—" He could only imagine how hellishly difficult it must have been for her. Yet, she had done it. "I didn't understand. I didn't know—"

"How could you? I didn't tell you. I should have. But, I was ashamed and I was afraid . . ."

"Despite that, you did try to tell me, didn't you?" Meade recalled the scene with painful clarity. "You tried, but I wouldn't listen. I said I didn't want to hear about it."

"I didn't try very hard," Brooke confessed honestly. "You—you seemed so angry, Meade—"

His mouth twisted as memory knifed into him. "I was more jealous than angry, Brooke," he said flatly.

"Jealous?" She had trouble believing this. "You were jealous of . . . Peter?"

He nodded, not proud of the emotion, but ready to admit to it.

"Why? How could you be—"

"Because you loved him. I know what he did to you, Brooke. But, before that. Before it went wrong, you *did* love him."

Had she, really? Brooke asked herself. She thought back to the first night she'd been in Meade's apartment and picked up the photograph of Sebastian and Gabrielle Browning. Even then, she'd wondered . . . doubted.

"Maybe I did, Meade," she replied slowly. "Or maybe it was the idea of him—the idea of getting married and having a family I truly loved. But whatever feelings I had for him—oh, Meade, they're nothing compared to the ones I have for you. *I love you.*"

"Enough to marry me?"

"More than enough!" she assured him with glowing eyes. "But, are you *sure*? Knowing—Meade, are you sure?"

"I'm very sure."

"It . . . it doesn't matter to you that I can't—?"

Meade gathered her hands like flowers and raised them to his lips, saluting the back of one and then the other. Their fingers twined together.

"It matters," he said frankly. "It matters to me because I understand it matters to you. If you hurt, I hurt, Brooke. But, if you're asking me if the fact that you're physically unable to conceive a child makes you any less womanly, any less desirable—oh, no, sweetheart. No."

Pulling Brooke against him, Meade kissed her. Their lips caught and clung, caught and clung, with languidly erotic adhesion. Meade's hard male mouth was cherishing as it moved against Brooke's ripely yielding one, making pledges and promises.

She opened to him, all softness and sighing pleasure. Her hands flowed up his arms and over his shoulders to delve into the hair at the back of his head. When he slid his tongue deep into her mouth, mimicking another even more intimate act of possession, her response was eager and ardent.

"We can have children in our life if we want them, Brooke," Meade told her huskily when he finally lifted his head. "We can adopt. I know it's more difficult today than it used to be, but there are children out there who need parents." A sudden frown furrowed his brow. "Before—when you were—did you ever consider adoption?"

Brooke ran her tongue over her kiss-bruised lips. "Oh, yes, I considered it. I went to agencies. I got information. Applications. I tried to show Peter, to get him interested. But he didn't even want to talk about it."

She paused, not really wanting to remember what had happened. Peter's reaction to the idea of adoption had been as painful for her to deal with as his reaction to her suggestion that they go to a fertility specialist had been. She recognized now that her ex-husband's sexual insecurities had more than matched her own.

"Brooke?" Meade prompted gently, seeing the hint of past grief on her face. He thought he could guess why Peter Livingstone had rejected the possibility of adoption.

"Peter said . . . he said he couldn't love a child that wasn't really his own. He said adoption would be an admission of f-failure. That, if he agreed to it, he'd always feel cheated." She gazed questioningly at Meade for several seconds. "Would you—?"

Something in the expression that settled over his strong features made Brooke think of Eleni O'Malley.

"No," he said simply. "I wouldn't feel cheated. I'd feel lucky."

"Lucky?" she echoed, knowing instinctively that his use

of the adjective had been a deliberate, not a random, choice.

He described himself as "lucky" to have found the right parents.

And his mother had described herself as "lucky" to have three children.

Could it possibly be? Was he telling her—

Meade watched Brooke's changeable emerald eyes grow wide. He answered the question he saw in their rain-forest depths even as he sensed her answering it for herself: "I'm adopted, Brooke. So are Kathleen and Mary Margaret."

"Adopted? You mean . . . your mother can't—couldn't—have children? Is *that* why she knew so much—"

He shook his head. "Whether it was my mother or father who couldn't, I don't know. I'm not even certain they do. I do know they both wanted children desperately and that they had a pretty rocky time in the first few years of their marriage when no babies came. They almost broke up completely at one point. But they found a way to work through it. Together." He ran one hand back through his hair. "I don't know why it never occurred to me to tell you. God knows, being adopted isn't something I'm ashamed of or try to hide. But, it's not really something I think about very much, either. You see, one of the many things my parents taught me when I was growing up is that making a baby is a matter of biology. Making a family is a matter of loving."

Brooke smiled very slowly. "Loving," she said softly, "is something I can do."

And reaching out, she tenderly curved her hand to fit the back of his neck, and drew his face to hers.

It was not the first time for either of them. Yet, as Meade swept her up in his arms and carried her off to his bedroom, Brooke had the sense that everything was wonderously new.

She began undressing him with trembling fingers. The buttons of his shirt gave way, one by one; then she opened the garment wide. She rubbed her palms against his broad chest as though anointing it with some precious oil. She combed her slender fingers through his mat of short, dark hair, seeking the thorn-hard buds that marked his male nipples. Brook drew her nails over the tightly furled nubbins of flesh and felt Meade shudder.

The tiny pearl fasteners that ran up the front of her demure white blouse were coaxed through their dainty loops. Meade peeled back her top as though unwrapping a priceless gift. His fingers skimmed her newly bared flesh, trailing ribbons of fire everywhere he touched.

It took him only a moment to undo and discard her bra, leaving her naked to the waist. He covered her high, firm breasts with his palms. Pressing gently, he massaged in a circular motion. She clutched at him, swaying like a willow in the wind.

He moved his hand downward.

The release of a button. The rasp of a zipper. A quick tug. Her trim linen skirt and the silky half-slip beneath fell to the floor. All that covered her from his gaze and touch were sheer taupe panty hose and a pair of lace-trimmed ivory briefs.

Meade went down on one knee. When he rose, Brooke was wearing nothing but a flush of sexual excitement.

The flush became her. Beautifully.

Brooke reached for the buckle of the black leather belt that spanned his narrow waist. When her fingers strayed for a moment, brushing provocatively against hard proof of his desire and need, his whole body tightened like a drawn bowstring.

Meade trapped her hand, pressing it flat against him for one throbbing moment. With his other hand, he caught a thick fistful of her silver-gilt hair. In a hoarse acknowledgment of her power over him, he groaned her name, then took her mouth with a devouring force that bordered on ravishment.

In the heartbeat after he finally tore his lips from her, he stripped off his trousers and briefs and cast them aside. Half in shadow, half in light, his body was magnificently male. Faultlessly toned sinew and muscle moved beneath taut skin. He was proudly, perfectly proportioned.

Brooke was drawn to him like iron to a magnet. Fit tight against him, she turned her face up to his, her eyes luminous with love and desire. He covered her mouth.

Locked together, they went down on his bed.

Kisses.

Swift and sizzling.

Long and lingering.

Enticing . . . exciting . . . endlessly erotic.

Brooke moved her head back and forth, her hair shifting against the same pillow she'd hugged in restless slumber the night before. Her lips parted invitingly. With hot, darting movements of his tongue, Meade caressed her. He nibbled and licked. Then, with an almost savage cry of hunger, he claimed the inner sweetness of her yielding mouth. She accepted his greedy exploration, making her own soft sounds of pleasure and need.

She let her hands roam over him freely . . . feverishly. She kneaded the proud power of his broad shoulders, the supple strength of his back, savoring the flex and feel of his body. She cupped the taut swell of his buttocks with daring palms and feathered the hollow at the base of his spine with delicately raking nails.

Their legs tangled. One of his thighs wedged between hers. The springy hair that downed his legs abraded her sensitive skin. Her muscles clenched of their own accord in a convulsive spasm of pleasure. She moved against him restlessly, a core of liquid heat radiating out from deep inside her. It coursed wildly through her veins, filling her with shimmering sensations of expectation.

A fine mist of perspiration sheened her fair skin. Meade feasted on the sweet-salt taste of it as he kissed a path from her mouth to her breasts. He teased one rosebud nipple with his tongue, circling, flicking, coaxing it to an aching, glistening peak. He lavished the same tribute on its eagerly pouting twin, then returned to take it deep into his mouth, suckling at it with a possessive, passionate rhythm.

There was nothing she would not do for him. Nothing she would not give. Every barrier had been brought down, every doubt cast aside. She loved him utterly . . . completely . . .

She tried to tell him, but the words came out as sobbing cries of pleasure. The one thing she could say was his name. She repeated it again and again. Burning currents swept through her.

There came an instant of exquisite, white-hot agony when to deny or delay became impossible. Attuned as he was to his love's every mood and movement, Meade knew when that moment came for Brooke.

Yet it was she who clasped the rigid length of him and guided him inside her. It was she who enclosed him by melting increments. It was she who sought and found the heavenly balance between giving and receiving.

In the last seconds, Meade rolled over onto his back. He brought Brooke with him, shifting her weight in an effortless movement until she lay atop him, her smooth, slender legs straddling his body.

Brooke arched up and back, hands pressed flat against the tangled bedclothes, her spine curving as she strained to deepen their union. She felt Meade's hands close about her hips, drawing her down against him while he thrust up.

The bonds of his control dissolved as he felt the first shudder of ecstasy take her. Her body tightened around him as ageless reflex took over. His palms slid from the curve of her hips to the lusher swell of her bottom.

"M-Meade—" Brooke's eyes closed and her head tilted

back, weighed down by the heavy tumble of her long hair. "Oh . . . oh . . ."

The world broke apart. No beginning. No end. Just an endless rapturous shattering. Yet, within that shattering, two people became one.

It was a moment of truth.

And an act of true love.

"I love you so much," Brooke said a long, long time later. She was lying partly on top of Meade, her hair spilling over her shoulders in a gossamer tumble. Her chin rested on her hands, which were stacked like cards against his chest.

"And I love you," Meade answered, charting the lovely line of her back with a lazy stroke of his palm. She was regarding him with eyes that seemed as tenderly green as a new leaf in spring. The curve of her ripe, rosy lips was warm and womanly.

Brooke sighed and shifted a little, letting her body move slowly against his.

Arching her foot, she ran her big toe up and down the side of his leg. She saw his mouth twist and turn up at one corner.

"When do you want to get married?" she asked.

"Mmmm . . . sometime after the honeymoon."

Brooke laughed, low and sweet. "And when do you want to have that?"

Meade's brows lifted and a mixture of heat and amusement sparked his eyes. "I thought we were having it," he returned.

A flush stole up Brooke's face, staining her cheeks pink. "Oh . . ." she said. She dipped her head and kissed the curve of his shoulder.

"That's just my opinion, you understand," Meade elaborated huskily, combing his fingers through her silken fall of hair. He made a sound that was, to Brooke's ears at least, half growl, half chuckle . . . all male satisfaction.

"Well . . . it's a very, um, good opinion," Brooke replied.

"Thank you." He tightened his grip on her a little and eased her upward along his body. Shifting, he nuzzled against the side of her throat, finding the spot where her pulse danced just beneath her skin. "When . . . mmm . . . when do *you* want to get married?" he questioned.

After a moment, Brooke lifted her head to look at him. She rubbed one finger against his chin. "Is tomorrow too soon?" she inquired mischievously.

His teeth flashed white. "You want to wait and be sure, hmm?"

Her expression turned dreamy yet determined. "I'm sure," she told him. "I'm very, very sure."

"So am I."

There was a lovely pause then, when no words seemed necessary.

"Can we get married in the gazebo?" Brooke asked finally, sensing the renewed stirring of his body with a deliciously feminine thrill.

"We can honeymoon there, too, if you'd like."

"Mmmm . . ." Memories warmed her.

"Too primitive?"

"Oh, not at all." She reflected a few seconds, a question that had nibbled at the edges of her awareness breaking through into her conscious thoughts. One corner of her mouth indented. "Speaking of primitive . . ."

"At your service."

"That music you were playing . . ."

"Ah. That. You like it?"

"I'd like to know what it is."

"What do you think it is?"

She put her tongue in her cheek and walked her fingers along the edge of his collarbone. "Hmmm-mmm . . . mmm . . ."

"Are you humming or trying come up with a title?" he teased.

"Meade—"

"Actually, it's a, ah, special collection."

"Greatest hits from the headhunters?"

"Not exactly."

"Am I getting close?" She moved one of her hands with wicked intent.

"Ah—ha! Yes . . . yes." She was getting close; he was getting hot—again.

"Tell me."

After a moment, he did. He wanted to laugh when he saw her eyes go wide and her face heat with a sudden surge of shyness that was so provocatively at odds with some of her other behavior.

"'M-Melodies to Mate B-by'?" she repeated. "Is that a direct translation?"

"A polite one."

"Oh . . ."

"Shocked?"

"No," she denied immediately, then hesitated for a moment. "To tell you the truth . . ."

"Please. Always."

She offered him a melting smile. "I, ah, thought it might be something like that the first night," she said slowly. "The music, I mean. Well . . . not actually *thought*. More like, ah—f-felt. Why . . . what made you play it again today?"

Meade drew a deep breath and let it out, realizing that there was no logical answer for this. "In a way, the music brought you to me that first night. I suppose . . . I suppose I hoped it would help bring you back."

"And you once told me you didn't believe in tribal magic," she chided.

"I told you I didn't *practice* it."

"*Do* you believe in it?"

"I believe in . . . miracles. I'm holding one." His eyes were as fond as they were fierce. "I love you, Brooke Livingstone. I love you . . . I love you . . ."

She told him the same thing.

"Meade?"

"Mmmm?"

"I think you should make a copy of that tape."

"Just one?"

"Well . . . one to put away and save."

"You have some future use in mind?"

"Mmm-hmm. Fifty years from now, when we're celebrating our golden anniversary together, I want to be prepared in case the band can't play our song."

EPILOGUE

THE NAME ON THE BIRTH certificate they received from the adoption agency read "Baby Girl Joy."

In Brooke's opinion, nothing could have been more appropriate.

She came home from work late one afternoon to find her husband napping on their bed with their six-month-old daughter asleep on his bare chest. The baby's arms and legs were splayed like a starfish and her diapered rump stuck up in the air. A silvery thread of drool beaded one corner of her rosebud mouth.

Smiling to herself, Brooke crossed quietly to the bed and sat down on the edge of the mattress. She stroked Joy's feathery dark brown curls for a few seconds, then felt her rounded bottom. She was about to whisper Meade's name when his eyes opened.

"You're home."

Bending, she kissed his brow. "Joy's wet," she said.

Meade's mouth quirked. "She's amazingly good at that," he commented wryly. Cradling the child, he sat up. The baby stirred a little, her pixie-perfect features wrinkling. A moment later, her nearly transluscent lids fluttered open. Her eyes were round and brown, like chocolate kisses.

"Well, hello," Brooke said softly. "And what did you and Daddy do all day?"

Joy's mouth opened in a huge yawn.

"Oh, thanks, Joy," Meade chuckled. Shifting the baby a little, he leaned over and gave Brooke a brushing kiss. "I'll change her, you change yourself."

"Deal," she agreed.

Five minutes later, she came into the nursery. Meade was by the baby's crib, looking down at Joy with an almost awed expression. Brooke came to stand beside him. He slipped an arm around her waist, drawing her close. After a moment, he turned his head and pressed his lips against her hair.

"She's beautiful, isn't she?" Brooke marveled.

"Takes after her mother."

She gave a low ripple of laughter. "Flattery will get you everywhere, Dr. O'Malley."

"Not flattery, sweetheart. Truth."

"Mmmm . . . right." She quivered a little as he thrummed his fingers against her side. "One of the things I'm going to have to warn Joy about when she gets older is to beware of Greeks bearing gifts of blarney."

It was his turn to laugh.

Brooke leaned her head against his shoulder. "Just what *did* you two do today?" she inquired.

"Oh, the usual. Slept. Ate. Burped. Wet. Went for a ride to the university and reduced Daddy's departmental chairman to a puddle of goo."

"Fun, hmm?"

"Terrific." He paused for a beat. "I turned down the field grant, Brooke."

Brooke looked at him, her eyes wide with surprise and pleasure. "You're not going away for the summer?"

Meade shook his head.

"You don't have to stay—"

"I want to."

"But—" Heaven knew, the idea of his leaving didn't make her happy, but she'd known when she married him that his work would require some separation.

"This is as much for me as it is for you and Joy, sweetheart," he assured her. "I like teaching. And, God knows, I've got more than enough lab work to keep me busy. Plus, I want to get the book finished." He slanted her a provocative glance. "Assuming, of course, I can figure out a way to please my very demanding in-house editor."

Brooke lifted her brows delicately. "Oh?"

"The woman's . . . mmm . . . insatiable. Never satisfied."

"Sounds terrible."

"Oh, I wouldn't say that . . ."

The kiss began lightly enough, but deepened to hungry intimacy when her tongue came in tantalizing search of his.

"Mmmm . . ." Brooke sighed. She melted against him, letting his strength support her. "Maybe if your editor didn't find you so distracting, the book would go faster," she suggested.

"You think so?"

"Could be . . ." She rubbed her cheek against his chest and circled his waist with her arms. "Won't you miss not going into the jungle this summer?"

"I've been going into the jungle for more than twenty years, Brooke. To tell the truth—" He paused, sorting through his feelings. Meade knew his instinctive need to explore, to "find out what's out there," would never go away. But the restlessness that had long possessed him was gone. His father had been right. He had needed a family of his own. "Maybe I'm getting old," he remarked wryly.

"Old!" Brooke looked up at him indignantly. She saw the glint in his eyes and realized he was only teasing. "A man who is thirty-five is *not* old, Archimedes Xavier

O'Malley!" she informed him with mock severity.

"That's reassuring to hear," he responded, grinning.

"And what's more, a man who can—" She rose on tiptoe and whispered in his ear. "Does that sound *old* to you?" she demanded.

"Actually, it sounds very, ah, inviting."

"So?"

"So what?" He began to fondle her through her clothes.

"So . . . what are you waiting for?" she asked throatily.

"Well, I don't want to go too fast . . ."

"M-Meade!" Brooke swayed.

"I love you, Brooke Livingstone O'Malley," he said, bending just enough to hook an arm beneath her wobbly knees. He scooped her up.

What happened next was, in Brooke's opinion, simply magic.

COMING NEXT MONTH

OVERNIGHT SENSATION #460
by Dianne Thomas
A fate arranged by her Great-Aunt Mercedes, Jessie finds herself in the constant company of TV idol Cam Holder, whose charm and good looks have her forgetting the very reason they were brought together...

THE SILENT HEART #461
by Kelly Adams
Laura Kincaid is more than striking—she is poetic, expressive, and hearing-impaired. Senatorial candidate David Evers surrenders his heart to her eloquence and fire. But her deafness has interfered before, and she's determined not to be hurt again...

BE SURE TO READ...

FOUL PLAY #456
by Steffie Hall
Handsome veterinarian Jake Elliott has already rescued Amy Klasse once; now her reputation's at stake. Will Jake be able to save it—and their newfound love, too?

THE RIALTO AFFAIR #457
by Jan Mathews
Two years ago, Dr. Amanda Pearson gave criminal lawyer Tyler Marshall more than the professional testimony he needed to win his case. Amanda had given herself, too. Now Ty's back—and he won't let her defense rest.

Order on opposite page